The Girl Next Door
Paperback Copyright © 2022 Lorhainne Ekelund
Editor: Talia Leduc

All rights reserved.
ISBN-13: 978-1998775118

Give feedback on the book at:
lorhainneeckhart@hotmail.com

Twitter: @LEckhart
Facebook: AuthorLorhainneEckhart

Printed in the U.S.A

# The Girl Next Door

## THE O'CONNELLS

**LORHAINNE ECKHART**

**Romance and suspense collide in this haunting romantic thriller.**

*When special forces operator Luke O'Connell meets a woman he never expected to see again, he uncovers the dangerous secret she is hiding and realizes the lengths someone will go to stop him from uncovering the truth.*

**Luke never in a million years expected to see Misty Bates again after a weekend of no strings and no names. But when his family introduces him to the nice girl next door, who turns out to be his mysterious fling, he soon figures out that the small-town girl is running from something, and uncovering it could destroy his chance at love.**

Luke O'Connell has been unlucky in love because of who he is. He has a job he can't talk about, with trouble always following him, and a peaceful night's sleep is something he can only dream of having.

The O'Connells step in and introduce him to Misty, a nice small-town girl, in the hopes that the two will hit it off, but what they don't know is that Luke and Misty have already met. Years ago, they spent a weekend together after a mission on the other side of the world. Luke is adamant he's not looking for a relationship, and he can't help seeing red flags behind Misty's nice-girl front. In her, he sees the kinds of ghosts people hide when they're running from something.

Luke doesn't like secrets, and there isn't a secret out there that he can't uncover. He soon discovers that Misty Bates used to be Chloe Welch, and she testified against a local hero after witnessing an unspeakable crime in which a house was burned down and a family perished. But when the small-town jury voted to acquit, the protection she had been promised by local authorities disappeared, and the suddenly hostile residents forced her to leave town.

Luke swears there can never be anything between him and Misty, but his digging has already put her in danger. Two cops show up on her doorstep with an arrest warrant, because the evidence in the case is suddenly pointing in her direction. Someone out there is trying to settle a score, and once again, the O'Connells find themselves deeply embroiled in a scandal, one that could ultimately endanger everyone in the family.

# CHAPTER

## One

Small and intimate was how Luke would have described Tessa and Owen's backyard, with its flowers, garden, and privacy. The wedding had been for just close friends and family. He had never seen his brother so happy, and as he leaned on the bar and watched a family he was finding it harder and harder to feel part of, he had to remind himself that his being alone wasn't his brother's fault.

"You're pretty quiet over here, drinking your beer, saying nothing, watching everyone."

He turned to take in Jack, his brother-in-law, who was now the governor of Montana. Four state troopers were present, one at the back gate, another in the yard over by Karen, and two in the small house. He knew that had to be giving the neighbors a lot to talk about. Jack lifted his hand as one of the troopers walked out of the house and over to him, then whispered something.

Jack wore his black suit as if it had been made for him. If Luke had been a girl, he'd have given his brother-in-law a second and third look, too. Jack wasn't as tall as he was, but he thought he might be prettier.

"Just enjoying a beer, Jack," he said.

Jack pulled his gaze, wincing into the sun. By the tug at the corners of his lips, Luke wasn't sure whether he was trying not to laugh or had something else on his mind, likely some humor at his expense. The trooper had walked off and now stood at the back door.

"I see you came alone, no girl on your arm," Jack said. He held a tumbler of bourbon, he thought. His one drink of the night, evidently, or maybe he'd live it up and have two.

Luke didn't even grunt, and he didn't pull his gaze. "Nope." He lifted his beer and downed the rest before putting the bottle on the bar and reaching behind it to pull another from a bucket of ice. He twisted off the cap and heard the sigh from Jack.

"You know everyone feels bad over what happened with Rosemary…"

There it was, that feeling, that sense of discomfort that settled right in the pit of his stomach. No one would let it go, yet he had. He allowed his gaze to settle on Jack with the practiced warning he gave to anyone who risked ending up on his wrong side.

"Is that why you came over, to counsel me about coming solo today?" Luke said. "All my siblings are now married, so should I have dragged some woman along with me? At least then you'd all be happy. Sure, I could have brought a plus one, but there would've been questions, a lot of questions, from my nosy family, and the poor girl doing me a favor would have been running before Owen and Tessa even said 'I do.' I'm not seeing anyone, am not involved, and don't plan on being so anytime soon. Rosemary couldn't have worked, anyway, so you just tell everyone to back off and let themselves off the hook. That was a momentary lapse, thinking someone like me could have something that resembled normal. Being a team guy, I know I can't have a girl waiting at home."

He let the words hang. Did the amusement on Jack's face mean he wasn't buying any of what Luke was saying or something else? That had been the most words Luke had strung together in a conversation with anyone in a long time.

"You know, you can keep telling everyone you're not meant for a relationship, but I know better than anyone that's not true," Jack said. "You should know that your sisters are likely going to take matters into their own hands. Just a heads-up."

He just stared at Jack, who was now leaning on the bar, staring into his tumbler. Something about the way he said it sounded like a warning. He knew something.

"And what matters would those be?"

From across the garden, his sister Suzanne was making a beeline over to them. Her long dirty-blond hair was wavy and styled, and her swelling belly in her gold and white maternity dress meant she was closer to having the baby than not. Harold, her husband of forty-five days, was following her .

"Oh, they figure they need to help you along toward happiness," Jack said. "You know your sisters."

Suzanne slid up beside him, linked her arm in his, and looked at his beer fondly. "You know, being pregnant, I absolutely miss that ice-cold beer. The taste…"

Luke just lifted a brow and glanced over to Harold. The man had been summoned and was evidently following orders, having reluctantly walked over for a friendly chat. His little sister did have a habit of getting her way.

"Well, you can just live vicariously through me as I enjoy this," Luke said. "So Jack was just giving me a heads-up that you and Karen are up to something, planning on sticking your noses into my life and doing something I'm not going to like. You know my life is my life. Don't be thinking you can fix me or—"

"Jack, you weren't supposed to say anything," Suzanne said. "Anyway, she's a nice girl. You'll like her. And it was Marcus who brought it up, so you can't give me and Karen all the credit. In fact, I think it was Jenny who mentioned it to Ryan first, or was it Tessa?"

His sister looked over to Harold. Now he knew why the man seemed so uncomfortable. He only lifted his gaze in a way that made Luke feel positive he didn't want to answer. "No idea, Suzanne. But Luke is right. You can't be trying to set your brother up. I told you before that this will backfire. Sorry, Luke. I told her. I'm just a bystander." He was holding a beer, his suit jacket gone and his white dress shirt sleeves rolled up.

Luke took in the wedding ring on his sister's finger, remembering the courthouse ceremony, five minutes to say "I do," sign the certificate, and walk out of City Hall. It had been quick, efficient, and nothing like the super romantic backyard celebration of his big brother. He hadn't expected this from Owen, but then, he really was head over heels for Tessa. Apparently, a guy would do anything for the girl he loved.

"I don't need you to find me a girl, Suzanne." Luke lifted his beer and took a swallow, then spotted Karen in a silky red dress that showed off all her curves. He didn't know who she was talking to, but her laughter drifted his way. His mom and dad were across the yard, too, with Alison and Bennett. The rest of the family and a handful of friends had turned this small and intimate event into the kind of party that should have made him happy. And he was happy—for Owen.

Suzanne was still holding his arm. "No, I'm sure you don't, but humor us, okay? Because sometimes we just know better. I think you'll agree when you meet her, and you'll actually thank us for sticking our noses into your life and wanting to fix you up." She fisted her hand and punched his arm playfully in that way of hers, though she really could pack a punch if she wanted to.

Harold lifted his gaze as if he'd already heard this, whereas Jack, he thought, was doing his best not to laugh at his expense. Luke stared down at his sister again, thinking she had too much time on her hands.

"You think you know what I need in my life more than I do? If we're sticking our noses into each other's lives, when is it my turn? I mean, you're due in a few weeks, and then what? Are you staying home to raise the baby? I guess that would be a win-win for Harold, wouldn't it? Kind of every guy's dream, having a barefoot housewife who'll have dinner ready for him when he gets home, keep his house clean, fetch his slippers, and not talk back."

Suzanne was staring daggers back at him. He knew full well which buttons to push and exactly what to say. Harold said nothing, though alarm flashed in his eyes, and he lifted his hands and stepped back as if wanting to take cover before the sparks flew.

Suzanne hissed, giving him a snarl that wiped her

smile away. "You're such an asshole sometimes," she snapped.

"You know what?" Harold said. "I think I hear Marcus calling me." Apparently, he had been smart enough not to wade into that dangerous territory with Suzanne, and he stepped back farther as if he couldn't believe Luke had brought it up.

Jack still appeared amused and was now shaking his head.

"Don't try spinning this back on me," Suzanne said. "You think I'm not used to how you fight, low and dirty? You toss out fighting words that you know will get under my skin and have me wanting to scratch your eyes out, except you know I'm more likely to slug you… Are you trying to mess with my head? Seriously, Luke, I'm not biting, not today. Tomorrow is a different story, though. Now I'm even more determined to mess with your life.

"And just FYI, after the baby is born, Mom and Charlotte have both said they're willing to step in and help out when I get back to work. And I will, because I've talked to Marcus several times about joining the department. He brushed me off the first three times, saying he can't hire me because I'm family, and Harold and I are married, but I pointed out to him that Charlotte worked there even after he and she were married. There's always the option of being a paramedic, or I could get back my job as a firefighter…"

Luke couldn't believe she'd said that. "The fire department you were fired from is not going to take you back, Suzanne," he said.

Even Jack, who was a master of not showing what he was thinking, seemed surprised. He was now leaning on the bar and hadn't pulled his gaze from Suzanne.

Luke could see his sister was still figuring things out. She'd really loved being a firefighter, but the politics had already decided she had to go.

"Look, I've heard over and over from Harold that there's no chance they'll take me back, but I'm persistent, and there is always a way. Yes, they scapegoated me, but I'm made of stronger stuff, persistence. I'll work the next department over. I've already reached out to the chief, and I still know people there, so I'm not about to take no for an answer. You can stop pushing my buttons with this 1950s 'back to the kitchen' thing. You think I don't know what you're doing, Luke, trying to spin this back on me so I'm not fixing you up? Well, it won't work, because she's already here."

He knew he was frowning, and he realized Jack wasn't surprised. He seemed to already know what was up. A smile had inched its way back into Suzanne's expression as if she was going to make this suddenly painful for him…

"She's here—like, in this backyard, at this wedding?"

Suzanne was really smiling now. She only nodded. Another glance to Jack, and he could see he knew who the girl in question was.

Luke found himself scanning the people, his family, Owen and Tessa's friends, then looked back to Suzanne. "And you…what, want to introduce me and expect some happily ever after? I'll pass."

She tapped his arm and then was somehow pulling him. Damn! For a pregnant woman, she was strong.

"Suzanne, what the hell…?" was all he said, letting his sister lead him across the yard. He spotted Marcus, the best man, dressed in a dark suit, his tie loosened, smiling as if he knew, too. So was Charlotte, wearing a frilly sleeveless blue dress.

"Oh, you just hush up and be nice," Suzanne said.

Ahead of them, Ryan wore a navy suit, standing beside Jenny, with her long dark hair hanging in soft curls. He stepped back to reveal the woman they were talking with, who had short red hair.

"Misty, this is my brother Luke, the one I was telling you about," Suzanne said as they approached.

She looked up, slender, short, wearing a soft green short-sleeved dress that hugged her curves. Luke felt that off feeling he'd had too many times before, taking in those full lips, her oval face, and those eyes, honey gold, a color he'd never forget. Her smile was there one minute, gone the next.

He just stared at her, remembering well the weekend they'd shared together. He felt someone slap his back, one of his brothers, and knew everyone was watching them.

"This is Misty Bates, Tessa and Owen's neighbor and friend," Jenny said.

Luke hadn't looked away. Misty hesitated and then seemed to pull herself together, holding out her delicate small hand. There was that smile again, with those dimples he remembered fondly.

"Hi, Luke. I've heard a lot about you from your family. It's nice to meet you."

So she was playing the game, not wanting anyone to catch on that they had already met. He could call her out or play along. He touched her hand, holding it, and hesitated, feeling the warmth and the unease. Evidently, she wasn't about to come clean.

"Since my family doesn't know how to stay out of

my business, how about we get a drink and exchange numbers?" he said.

He thought it was Marcus who made a rude noise. Luke somehow manoeuvred Misty back to the bar, where Jack was no longer standing, holding out his arm as he walked with her. She wore killer heels, which showed off legs he remembered well.

*One, two, three…* He had counted their footsteps in his head until they were far enough away from everyone. The tall, lanky bartender was opening a bottle of red wine and glanced at her, saying, "What can I get you?"

"I'll have a glass of that red," she said.

Luke waited for the bartender to pour it. "You know what I remember, Misty, about the last time I saw you?"

She stood so stiffly, lifting her chin as she flicked those eyes at him. He swore he could get lost in them. She said nothing for a moment as she took the glass from the bartender and sipped. "Okay, I'll bite," she replied. "What?"

Luke waited for the bartender to walk away, well aware that everyone in his family was watching them. "One of the best no-strings weekends of my life. But I never expected to see you again. Small world, Misty. Greece is a long way from Livingston."

She only nodded. "It is, at that. So tell me, Luke, when did you join the military? Because I'm pretty sure that when we spent the weekend together, I knew you as a man named Henry who worked for a software company in California, not as Luke O'Connell."

It had been during one of his missions on the other side of the world, when he played the role of someone else. He really hadn't expected to see her again.

"Well, I guess you know I lied. Should I apologize?" He knew he sounded like an asshole.

She lifted a brow. "For lying about who you were or for the no-strings weekend? If I recall, we both agreed. Sure, I could be angry, but instead, let's stand here for a few more minutes and pretend to talk while I drink my wine, and then I'll make my way back over to your family and make my excuses, tell them I'm not interested, that you're not my type or something like that." She was so damn matter of fact.

And she was giving him an out. But there was just something about her, something that seemed different from the woman he had spent that weekend with in Plaka.

"Does that mean you're not up for another no-strings weekend?" he said.

She could have slapped him. Instead, she pulled in a breath and seemed to consider something, lifting her glass to her lips.

Suzanne strode over and slid her hand over Misty's arm before she could answer him. "So are you two hitting it off?" she said.

Of course his sister couldn't leave it alone. The smile was pasted back on Misty's face now, the one that reminded him of a nice girl, but he realized that easy smile was only a front.

She let out a soft laugh. "Luke is great. It was really nice to put a face to the name after all I've heard. But I'm going to make my way back…" She gestured behind her to where Ryan, Jenny, Charlotte, and Marcus were, then lowered her wine and started walking away.

That left him and Suzanne, who was now staring daggers his way again. "What did you say to her, Luke?"

He just took in his sister, then lifted his beer, watching as Misty talked with Jenny and Charlotte. When she looked his way, he realized maybe there was a reason she didn't want anyone to know they'd already met. There was just something about her…

"We just chatted for a minute, Suzanne, until you interrupted," he said.

Suzanne frowned and tapped his arm. "Do you need me to drag you back over there?"

He only shook his head and looked back over to Misty, who was laughing at something Charlotte had said. He knew when a woman was avoiding looking his way. What was it about her? It seemed secrets and lies were just what he attracted.

"Nope," he said. "I already told you I'm not looking for a relationship, Suzanne, and she's not really my type." He hoped she would drop it.

"So what exactly is your type, Luke?"

There it was, the million-dollar question. All he did was lift his beer and take another swallow as he realized Misty Bates was looking right at him.

He knew nervousness.

He knew avoidance.

And he knew Misty Bates had displayed both since the moment Suzanne walked him over, the moment they'd met again.

He watched the redhead from a distance as the night settled and the party wound down. The bride and groom had now left for their honeymoon in Grand Turk, a gift from all of them. It was a place he'd been too many times to count, but his brother and his new wife would see the areas tourists did, not the real island, which Luke and his team understood.

He carried the last of the dishes into the house and took in his mom, Alison, and Cassie as they put some order back into the kitchen. Ryan, Harold, and Marcus were still outside, drinking a beer and talking, whereas Charlotte was carrying a tired Cameron and leading Eva to the back door.

"Getting ready to leave?" Luke said. "The kids look like they're done."

She shot him a look. "Oh, this one is past tired." She patted Cameron's back as he rubbed his eyes. "Just going to grab Marcus. Time to takes these ones home and put them to bed. Oh, and it's not too late, you know. Misty is getting ready to leave. Jenny is there with her. You should walk her home. It's the gentlemanly thing to do."

Cassie and Alison glanced his way, smiling, teasing, and he knew they wanted to add something. Charlotte glanced past him to the door, where Misty and Jenny were, and her brow crooked. His sisters and sisters-in-law had become quite the pack, trying to arrange his love life. She laughed softly before walking out back, where he spotted his dad and Brady heading around the side of the house. He wondered what that was about, but then, he hadn't really had a chance to catch up with anyone before the wedding.

He took one step and then another to the front door, which was now open. Jenny was hugging Misty goodbye. Too small a world, considering the woman he had never planned to see again after their weekend sex marathon was actually a hometown friend of his family. What were the odds? He was still trying to wrap his head around it, especially the fact that she hadn't called him out for using a fake name and alias.

"I heard you were leaving," he said as he came to a stop beside Jenny, who rested her arm on his suit jacket. "Why don't I walk you home?"

Misty hesitated, shaking out the black sweater she had been holding over her arm and pulling it on.

"That's a great idea, considering it's now dark out," Jenny said, jumping in before Misty could say no or Luke could add anything else to make this more awkward. "It will give you two a chance to talk."

Misty only smiled and said nothing as he followed her out the door. She started down the gravel walkway, the only landscaping Owen and Tessa had done out front. He held his arm out to her, taking in those killer heels. He wondered at times how women could walk in them. She hesitated only a second before taking his arm.

"Well, you didn't have to walk me. I live right here. In case I need to remind you, it was no strings, never seeing each other again. Please feel free to ignore me."

"And what, pretend I'm not interested?" he said. "You forget I've seen you naked. Seems rather awkward, considering you're now friends with the women in my family. In case you haven't noticed, they've gone to quite the lengths to push us together, and they're going to keep sticking their noses in because they have it in their heads that we're perfect for each other. What would they think if they only knew we'd already met? How many years has it been?"

He could feel her fist her hand on his arm as they walked down the sidewalk, past the overgrown hedges. He took in her single-story bungalow, which was almost identical to Tessa and Owen's.

"You're not saying anything. Should I be insulted?" he said. He didn't know what to make of her, but he could feel when someone was uncomfortable.

"Oh, I remember how long ago it was. A little over three years, I think. But I'll talk to Tessa when she's back, and Jenny as well, and tell them we're just too different or something along those lines, and it could never work. They'll drop it, so don't worry. And they'll never push again. But then, I don't think you want them knowing I was just one of your many conquests. A man like you, Luke, with a false name, a false identity…

Pretty sure you play with a lot of women, don't you? No strings."

He could feel her shrug. He didn't think he should answer her. He was by no means a saint, and there were only a few women he didn't think he'd ever forget. Why was he seeing shadows around everyone now? It was likely because of what he did.

"So when we met at that outdoor café in Plaka, were you living here? Were you already friends with—"

"Tessa?" She jumped in before he could finish. "I'm friends with Tessa because she bought the house shortly after I bought this one. We met over the fence, chatted, talked, and we've been good friends ever since. Tessa introduced me to the rest of your family—and I have to say, you have a nice family, Luke. Now, as I said, I'll make excuses, and you won't have to worry about them pushing us together again. But I'm not interested in hooking up with a player. And you are a player, Luke." She gestured toward him as they strode across the grass to the front door, where the outside light was off.

"You should leave a light on so you don't come back in the dark," he said.

She pulled her hand free from his arm as she stepped up on the stoop, pulled open the screen door, and grabbed her keys from her small purse. He took in the two deadbolts and the heavy front door, not something the average person would notice. She had two different keys, too. She shoved one in and unlocked the heavy door, then opened it just a bit and turned to him, the darkness lingering.

"Well, thank you, Luke, for walking me home."

That was it. That was all she said. She stood there in the darkness, not even reaching inside to turn on the light, and that had him thinking she was hiding something.

"You never answered me before about another no-strings weekend," he said. "You should invite me in."

She didn't smile, but there was something in her expression. She looked away for a second, hesitated, and shook her head. "No, Luke. Even though I was completely, one hundred percent complicit in our no-strings weekend, I will not have a repeat. It was all I wanted then. We were two strangers on the other side of the world, attracted to each other, but it was just sex. For a moment, it was what I needed, being someone else, doing something wild and crazy that I wouldn't normally do. But here we are, back in reality, where I live. And I'm friends with your family, so if it's all the same to you, I'd like to leave that moment in time, that weekend we shared, where it is. Let's not mention it or talk about it. And, to be clear, it won't ever happen again. Goodnight, Luke."

She stepped inside while he held the screen, then closed the inside door in his face before he could add anything.

He listened to the sound of the deadbolts locking. As he stepped back, letting the screen door close, a faint light flicked on, and he dragged his gaze to the front window, where heavy curtains were drawn. The blinds were closed on the other windows, too.

Something wasn't right here. Something was off. She had walked into a darkened house, heavily secured, with curtains drawn and blinds closed. No one did that unless she had something to hide, something inside that she didn't want anyone to see.

Luke strode to the edge of the front yard, across the

grass, and took in the side of the small house. Memories of his weekend with the redhead were coming back to him, every kiss, every touch, every moment they had spent together.

He wondered now what it was about her that had him seeing shadows and ghosts.

"I thought I heard you out here," said Raymond O'Connell, wearing an old T-shirt and sweats, his hair sticking up as he reached for the coffeepot. Surprisingly, his dad had managed to maintain his other identity, Jake from California, boyfriend to his mother, who had somehow convinced him to stay in Livingston because it was better for her.

Better for his mom meant not spending months away from her children and grandchildren. He'd never expected Raymond to give in the way he had, considering danger could always be one step away.

"It's morning, quiet, just the way I like it," Luke said.

The sun was just coming up, and the sound of the birds from the open kitchen window was the only thing he wanted to hear in the morning. He stared at his open laptop on the island in front of him, then took in his dad, whose dark hair was filled with more and more gray every day. Raymond took a swallow of coffee and leaned against the sink, not pulling his gaze. Apparently, he had something on his mind.

"I take it Mom is still asleep," Luke said. Knowing his mom was happy now, no longer alone, made him unsettled in a way it shouldn't have. Maybe it was because it seemed everyone had someone except him. That misery loves company was a fact he was becoming too familiar with, though he wouldn't have admitted it to anyone.

"She is," Raymond said. "You already know she's made it clear she's not leaving Livingston. I'm not sure how comfortable I am, but I'll take it a day at a time, I guess, for your mom, at least for the foreseeable future. She has plans for today, wanting to drag me along to Suzanne's to make sure she has everything she needs and to fuss over her. She's counting down the days until Suzanne has the baby. Our baby having a baby…" His dad's face softened as if he was sinking into his family happiness. "She's really digging her heels in about not leaving. Then there are Eva and Cameron, and I think she's made some plans with Alison today, too. She'll likely also have some questions for you about that redheaded friend of Tessa's everyone was convinced you needed to meet and settle down with."

His dad gestured to the secure laptop. He was searching for Misty Bates, but that name wasn't coming up anywhere. She had no social media or anything on the internet.

"You know, my private life is just that," Luke said. "I'm not interested in being fixed up. When or if I meet someone, it will be on my terms, not because my nosy siblings want to set me up on a blind date. They're trying to make me fit in, get me a wife and kids, but you know I'm not exactly the poster boy for domesticity." He closed the laptop and slid his mug over, then gestured to the coffeepot. His dad must have understood, as he reached to pour him a cup just as he heard footsteps.

His mom appeared, wearing a housecoat. "What's this about being a poster boy?"

So she had heard what he'd said. His dad had already reached for a mug and poured her a cup as well, and she settled in beside him. Luke could see how much they really loved each other from the way she was looking at him. Then she glanced at Luke. Her short dark hair was a mess, and tiny lines deepened around her eyes as she narrowed her gaze.

"Luke, you think I don't know that you couldn't take your eyes off that friend of Tessa's? Did you ask her out after you walked her home? Very chivalrous, by the way."

His dad only grunted in response. He could feel the scrutiny.

"What do you know about this Misty Bates?" Luke said. "I mean, she and Tessa are neighbors, friends, but how well do you all know her? Where's she from? What skeletons are in her closet?"

His dad could hide everything he was thinking, but by the way he narrowed his gaze, not looking away, he had clearly figured out there was more to the situation than met the eye. "You seeing ghosts there, Luke? Sometimes a nice girl is just that."

Maybe his mom realized what Raymond was getting at. She hesitated before saying, "Luke, I don't know her that well, but I know Tessa, Jenny, Suzanne and Charlotte are all friends with her, and your brothers too. They say she's a nice lady, just a nice hometown girl. She's never been in trouble and is always pleasant, with a great sense of humor. What is this? Why are you looking to dig up her skeletons? Sure, everyone has secrets of some kind, but it sounds as if you're trying to find a reason you can't like her. Is that what you're doing, Luke, trying to find something on her to vindicate yourself? Maybe we should talk about you and everything you've done and still do for the military, the things you can't and don't talk about. Maybe the skeletons you're worried about are your own."

He had never expected his mom to go off on him like that, and he didn't much like feeling the scrutiny. They were waiting for him to answer.

If he told them the truth of how they'd really met, their no-strings weekend, would his mom still say she was the nice girl next door? Or would she side with him and say he was right, that she was no good?

If she did the latter, he'd probably find a way to see her. He really was a sick bastard.

"I'm just saying, how well do you really know someone?" he said. "I mean, what does she do? Has she been in trouble? She's not married, so are there crazy exes in the wings? What do you really know about her past, where she comes from, her parents, her family, where she grew up, and everything she's done?"

His dad raised his brows, and Luke was pretty sure there was amusement there. Raymond gestured toward him. "Okay, now I'm starting to figure out what this is really about: Rosemary. You know, I can tell you've been doing what you do for so long that you automatically look for the darkness in someone now, believing deep, dark secrets are hiding everywhere. But not everyone has something to hide, son. You may be seeing ghosts and problems when there aren't any—unless you know something about her that the rest of the family doesn't. Is there something? Or are you trying to find the reasons you can't be happy? Because I'm telling you from experience, if you look hard enough, you can find a reason with anyone. Don't do that to yourself."

His mom glanced to her dad and then back to Luke. He could see the questions she likely had, but he said nothing as she stepped forward and rested her mug on the island. "You know what, Luke? I would like to ask you to do something for me."

The way she stood there, he could see the determination. For a moment, he didn't want to agree, because it seemed he could be walking into something. Why was it that he suddenly felt as if his parents were trying to steer him in an unwanted direction?

"And what would that be?" he said.

"I want you to ask Misty out on a date. Tonight. And," she continued with emphasis when he went to cut in, "I want you to just enjoy yourself, talk to her, have dinner, a beer, something. But it should be an honest to goodness date, where no one can tell you what to do. And you will stop this nonsense of trying to dig up something in her past."

Maybe it was the way Iris and Raymond seemed to be tag-teaming him that had him wanting to roll his shoulders, to fidget, which he never did. His mom inclined her head, her lips firmed. He was seeing a new side of her, that determination.

"And then what?" he said. "If I ask her out on a date, you'll drop this?"

A smile touched his mom's lips, and she shrugged. "Just call her," she said. She pulled open the drawer and produced an old address book, which she flipped open and set on top of his closed laptop. "There's her number." She pressed her finger to the page.

He wondered whether his mom might even pick up the phone for him and start dialing. It was just a feeling he had. He'd never expected this from her.

"On one condition," he said. He could see amusement in the way his dad smiled.

"And that is?" His mom didn't sound impressed.

"If I call her and take her out, you can't ask about her, bring her up, or try to set me up again. And," he added with emphasis, "you will make sure everyone in the family backs off. No asking how the date was, no working an angle, no pushing me about taking her out again or suddenly forcing her into my path. Nothing. You agree to all that, and I'll call her."

He actually pulled out his phone. His dad tried to hide his amusement by pulling his hand over his face, and he could hear the scratch of his whiskers. His mom, he could see, was having a lot of trouble with his terms. Maybe she hadn't expected this.

She set a hand on her hip before looking over her shoulder to his dad, who only gestured toward Luke. When she looked back at him, he could see the determination. "You want to make that deal with me, with your brothers and sisters, then you have to be one hundred percent present on your date. No cutting the night short or making excuses or spending the night trying to spin theories about why she isn't for you. You will not and cannot have it in your head that it isn't going to work. You have to be open to her, talk to her, listen to her. You will be all in on your night out with Misty, or no deal."

His mother wasn't about to let him have the upper

hand in this. For a second, he took in her extended hand, considering. He hesitated only a second before shaking it. "Fine. I agree. But have you ever thought that just maybe, Misty herself may not be interested in me?"

# CHAPTER

## Four

He could have called, but showing up on her doorstep seemed like the wiser choice. He couldn't shake the feeling that he was missing something about Misty Bates. He had questions, a lot of questions, as he stood on the sidewalk in front of her house.

His brother's place seemed so quiet with Owen and Tessa gone, yet so did Misty's house, where the curtains and heavy blinds were still closed. Was he just seeing ghosts? Maybe she liked her privacy. Maybe he needed there to be something wrong with her so he could justify to himself why he couldn't be happy.

But then, wasn't it true that the first thing someone did when hiding was close up everything, make sure no one could see in?

He took in the midday sun and heard the ding of his phone. When he pulled it from his pocket and checked the screen, there was a text from Jess.

*Who is Misty Bates? What do you want to know, work or personal?*

He smiled. His Googling had come up with nothing on the woman, yet it seemed everyone now plastered everything across social media: their photos, their personal lives, even things no one should ever see. But not Misty. She didn't seem to exist.

He typed a quick text back. *Everything you can find. She's just a girl next door. Family is trying to do the matchmaking thing. Find out what she was doing in Plaka three years ago.*

He glanced to the closed door and back to the phone when he saw the thumbs-up in reply, knowing Jess would dig and find things the average person couldn't. At least his team leader wouldn't accuse him of being paranoid and looking for ghosts. The rest of the team saw the same bad things, the same secrets, that he did. It meant expecting the worst in everyone, which was the one thing he couldn't do if he wanted a healthy, happy relationship.

But then, Luke and his team didn't have perfect all-American families waiting for them at home. He still wondered how his own dad managed it, after doing what he did and being who he was.

Luke walked up the front walkway, taking in the small paving stones that led to the house. The front was bare, with no flowers, nothing special that would draw attention. It was just a house with no personality. The door was closed, and he took a second to just listen, but he heard nothing.

He pulled open the screen, fisted his hand, and knocked. The seconds ticked by, and he thought he saw movement from inside. He knew the curtain had moved, but someone was being careful. Then he heard footsteps and the sound of the two deadbolts, and he couldn't help wondering how his family hadn't thought that was odd in any way.

The door opened a crack, and he spotted a bare hallway behind her. Her short red hair was damp and her face free of makeup, and she wore a black T-shirt and jean shorts. The day was warm, but by the way her honey-brown eyes flashed, she wasn't happy to see him.

"Luke, what are you doing here?"

Her hand was on the door, and the motion told him she didn't want him coming in. He wondered now whether Tessa or anyone from his family had ever been inside. For a second, he wished he'd called Ryan, Jenny, Marcus, Charlotte, or, better yet, nosy Suzanne and questioned them more about how Misty lived. Had they ever been over at her place? What did they know about her past?

"Are you just going to stand there, staring at me, or are you going to say something?" she said.

He let out a rough laugh under his breath, pulled off his sunglasses, and tucked them in the front of his gray T-shirt. "My family really wants us together, apparently, but it seems you're the one I'm going to have to convince. I found myself roped into asking you out this morning, so how about it?"

She stared up at him in disbelief, and for a moment he wasn't sure she'd answer. "No," she finally said with emphasis. "First, that's not how you ask a girl out. You were roped into it? Really, Luke?" She let out a soft laugh, but she still hadn't moved, and he could see she wasn't about to make this easy.

"You realize my family will keep pushing…"

"I told you last night that I would make sure your family understands I'm not interested, so you're off the hook," she said. Then she went to step back, and he knew the door was about to be closed in his face again. He slapped his hand to it.

"Hey, just wait a second," he said. "I'm starting to pick up on something that has me wondering if there's more to you than I would've thought. I don't know. It just seems as if you're trying to hide something."

She let out a sigh. "And what would that be, Luke?"

"Well, that's the thing. I don't know. Are you hiding something, Misty? Because I'm wondering a lot of things as I look at you, at how you're acting. Tell me, why is it that you have everything closed up here, curtains and blinds so no one can see in? Then there are the double deadbolts on the door. Are you scared of someone? Are you running, hiding?"

He could see her thinking. Her mouth opened as if she was going to say something, but then she didn't. She was nervous. Something was off.

"What, because I'm not interested in a repeat of what happened with a man who couldn't even use his real name, I'm suddenly hiding something? Maybe I should be asking you the same questions, Luke. I mean, why the fake name? Why the fake identity? You're in the military—the army, is it? I don't really know, because your family didn't elaborate, which has me wondering what you were really doing in Plaka. I mean, look at you. You don't look like some grunt. Maybe I should be asking what you're hiding, what you're really about.

"You know what, Luke? I'm not interested, so if you don't mind, I'd really like it if you'd not show up again. I'm sure you don't want your family knowing how we met and how you lied to me. So if it's all the same to you, please take your hand off my door and go away. No is no. I will not go out with you, and I will not have you questioning me. Instead, maybe you should take a long, hard look at yourself in the mirror." She really was going off on him, going over the top in her anger.

"You're deflecting, Misty, and your outrage is straying into defensiveness. You ever invite my family into your place? It's not lost on me that you haven't answered me about this Fort Knox thing you have going on. Yeah, I know hiding, and I know secrets. You know what I do? It's the kind of job where a secret doesn't stay secret for long. I can dig and find out all kinds of secrets about someone that the average person would never learn. The skeletons. Do you have skeletons lurking behind those curtains? Are you in trouble? Did you do something, or are you hiding from something?"

She paled, and her eyes flickered with emotion. When his phone dinged, he didn't pull it from his pocket at first. He was standing in front of her, seeing the kind of fear on her face that told him he was treading right into something she didn't want him to see.

When he finally glanced at his phone, keeping his hand on the open door, he saw a text from Jess.

*You were right. Found something. Call me. Maybe ask her who Chloe Welch is.*

But something about being right in these circumstances didn't make him happy.

"Please go, Luke," she said. Her voice was low, nervous.

"Sure. But first, tell me who Chloe Welch is."

She let go of the door. For a moment, she looked as if the rug had been yanked out from under her. Whatever it was Jess had found, evidently, Chloe Welch was at the center of what Misty was hiding.

"You're an asshole," Misty said.

Luke filled a glass with water and took in the sparse furnishings of the small older house. A sofa sat in the living room, with its dated brown paneling, and there was no table in the green and brown kitchen, only two bar stools at the island. Misty was perched on one, her elbows resting on the speckled brown laminate countertop, her head in her hands. He couldn't see her face. She was hiding.

"Here, drink this." He set the glass down, and she reached for it, then looked up at him. He shrugged. "You think I haven't been called that and worse? The thing about me, though, is that I push and dig until I find what I'm looking for. I had a feeling you were hiding something. So who is this Chloe Welch? You want to tell me, or do I need to make a call and find out what you're hiding?"

As he pulled his cell phone from his pocket, Misty glanced to it and sat stiffly. She lifted the glass and took a swallow of water, then took her time resting it back on the counter.

"Last chance." He knew he was pushing.

"Chloe Welch is me," she said.

Okay, that he hadn't expected.

"Excuse me? You're Chloe?"

She only nodded, then tilted her head. "You have someone digging into my life? Why?"

"Already told you I don't like secrets, and I knew there was a big red flag with you. So you're Chloe. Why the name change? What did you do? Who are you hiding from? Does anyone in my family know?"

She tensed, her jaw stiff, and for a moment he wondered whether he should just phone Jess and find out everything. It would be simpler, more to the point. He could walk out the door and be done there. And then what? He'd tell his family he was right?

For reasons he couldn't have explained, he just couldn't do that. Maybe it was the weekend he'd had, or his siblings' fondness for her, or the fact that she was the nice girl next door, but he needed her to explain everything. He wanted her to come clean to him.

"As far as anyone knows, I'm Misty and have been for a long time. I mean, evidently, I don't need to explain to you why a person changes her name."

He held her gaze. How deeply was she steeped in trouble? "Did you do something? Are you hiding? Why would you change your name unless you've done something and need to hide?"

She pulled in a breath. "I don't want to be found, if that's what you're asking. No, I didn't do the kind of thing you're thinking. Or maybe I did, because I don't know what you're thinking. The way you're looking at me, I feel as if I'm the worst of the worst, as if I did something, when it was really the other way around. Let's just say I saw something and tried to do the right thing, but I ended up coming forward about the wrong kind of person.

"No one here knows. That's why I moved here for a fresh start when everything blew up in my face. Your family doesn't know, and I'd rather they didn't. I have a good life here, and I want it to stay that way. I like being happy, Luke, and I like being Misty. I don't suppose you could just walk out that door and forget you heard that name?"

He realized she was serious. He shook his head. "No, sorry. I can't, or I won't. Tell me what happened. Start at the beginning." He was still holding his phone, seeing another text from Jess.

*You there??*

He sent a quick text back: *Yeah. Call you soon. With Chloe now.*

Maybe she knew the message was about her, as she glanced away. He wondered what she was thinking. Had she been running when he met her in Plaka?

"I used to live in a small Wyoming town, and I saw something I wasn't supposed to see," she said. "Because I believed in doing the right thing, I came forward to the police, the small-town police, who I believed would see justice done. But the world doesn't work that way, and I soon discovered that.

"I had seen a man running from a house before it caught fire. It was arson. The family was inside, and they all died. There were two little kids, four and six.

That was what made me come forward. It should've been an open and shut case, but the man was a local hero by the name of Dirk Randall. He'd saved a kid from drowning when he was a teenager—and not just any kid but the son of a retired senator. So he was given a medal, you know, the ones towns and cities give out when you do something heroic for someone who matters. Do you want me to go on?"

He put his cell phone down on the island. It seemed she'd walked into the kind of situation that could've ended up with someone gunning for her. "Yes, go on." He gestured toward her. "You came forward and said what no one wanted to hear, and you were run out of town."

She only stared at him, confusion in her honey-brown eyes. Her brows knit. "No. The police, the sheriff, and the deputies were all over it. In fact, they arrested him, and I was the key witness for the DA. But having a senator in your corner, and the kind of political and legal power that comes with that, had the defence team coming at me. I mean, these were good lawyers, a dream team that could spin anything, the kind of lawyers I would never be able to afford.

"They were so good that if I hadn't seen what I had, I'd likely have believed the story they spun. I was cross-examined on the stand in a courtroom, questioned for two days. My entire life was put on trial, my character assassinated, and every piece of dirt they could find on me was dug up, including the fact that I had stolen a pack of gum from the drug store when I was six. The owner caught me and I was grounded for, like, a year. Then there were the times in high school that I had tried pot or beer, or the time I punched the girl who'd been making eyes at my boyfriend in the face.

"I was basically made out to be a thief, a liar, a tramp, and don't forget a drug addict. Even though I'd never met Dirk, my credibility was destroyed. It was alleged that I was jealous, trying to hurt a young man who had saved someone of importance. So who do you believe? I'm a good person. I can remember saying that over and over on the stand as everything about me was twisted. No one bothered to talk about how I volunteered at the animal shelter, or how I picked up the elderly during the election when they had no other way of getting to the polls to vote. I paid my taxes, paid all my bills, even ran after people who dropped money to give it back to them. I was happy. But that side of me, who I was, no one saw it.

"I had some of the best lawyers gunning for me, destroying my character. Every question they asked was spun in a way that it wouldn't matter what I said, because for a moment, even I started to believe I was a horrible person." She lifted her hands as if they were a scale. "So you have jurors watching the show and deciding who to believe, the lying tramp or the local hero who risked his life. Reasonable doubt was all they needed, and the small-town jury voted unanimously to acquit, without a doubt.

"When I came forward, I was treated like a hero for speaking up, but suddenly, all the protection the cops had promised disappeared. I was seen as the enemy. The town I grew up in turned hostile, and I was forced to leave. So yes, Luke, when you met me in Plaka, I had sold everything I owned and taken a trip as far away from that small town as I could, to a place where no one knew my name. And you know what I learned after that no-strings weekend? In becoming Misty Bates, I suddenly had a chance at a new life. No one saw me as the person who'd accused a local hero. I moved to Livingston, Montana, because it's not Wyoming, and for the three years I've been here, I haven't had any whispers behind my back.

"I haven't been called a liar. I haven't had my car tires slashed or had 'whore' written with a Sharpie on my car door. I haven't had any notes left in my mailbox, threatening my life, threatening to violate me. I was scared, because when you're suddenly seen as guilty, as a liar, you stop sleeping, stop eating. I didn't know if I would walk into my house to find some crazy person waiting to exact justice. I was seen as someone who would lie about a man, a local hero, someone who had done more for the community than anyone..." She pulled in a breath.

His phone dinged again.

"What is it?" she said.

He picked it up and just shook his head.

*Call me,* Jess had written. *It can't wait, because the name was flagged.*

He dialed and said, "Do you know why your name would be flagged in the system?"

She didn't answer, but he didn't miss the alarm in her expression.

Jess answered before the phone had finished ringing once. "It's about time," he said. "What the hell are you stepping into?"

"Well, you know me. What's going on?"

"This Misty Bates used to be Chloe Welch. I found her through ViCAP. Her name was flagged, something about a fire, arson. A family perished. It's pretty bad shit, and she's wanted for questioning."

He wondered, as he looked over to Misty—or was it Chloe?—whether she had any idea. "Who's looking for her?" he said. "Is it a warrant?"

Maybe she understood, as her face paled again.

"Local cops in Cody, Wyoming," Jess said. "You should have told me, because her name is flagged, so the moment I started looking, my inquiry triggered something. There's nothing about a warrant, but you know that doesn't mean anything. That she's a person of interest means they have something. You said you're with her? You know her? What do you want me to do?"

He only shook his head. "Find out why she's a person of interest, what they have. Thanks for the heads-up," he said.

He knew Jess would do more than that, anyway. As he rested his phone on the counter, he took in the redhead he'd spent the most incredible weekend with, who had ghosts and secrets that were very real.

If his family only knew the truth.

"Well, say something, please, Luke, because you're scaring the hell out of me," she said. "A person of interest? A warrant? What does that mean?"

He wondered for a moment what she wasn't telling him. "I think you know what it means. It seems you're in a hot mess, Chloe. Can I call you Chloe?"

She shut her eyes, and when she opened them, he could see the fury, the fear. "Seems we're beyond that, aren't we? So what is it, Luke? Level with me. What kind of trouble am I in? Because I don't know."

"Seems you're wanted for questioning, so either you didn't tell me everything, because it sounds like the cops are looking at you for the fire, or they're coming after you because the local hero's lawyers were so good that they've got the spotlight shining on you now. Or maybe you lied and made the whole thing up. So which is it, Chloe? Because as I see it, you've pissed off the wrong person."

# CHAPTER
## Six

" I 'm not sure what you're accusing me of," Chloe said. "This is insane. Every day I wish I didn't see what I did. I wish I didn't see Dirk Randall walking out of that house. But it was him. The only thing I didn't do, and I wish I did, was take a photo on my phone—but then, as good as his lawyers were, they likely would've gotten that tossed out, as well. The way you're standing here in my house, making me feel like a criminal…" Her hand was shaking.

He could see she was fast moving to a place of fear and anger, which he knew well from both sides. "I'm not saying you're guilty of the crime. All I said is you're hiding something. Secrets and lies are things I know well. I don't like them, especially around my family."

"So you just had to dig into my private life? What gives you the right, Luke?" She was pissed off.

The way she stared at him, so accusing, he wondered why he'd felt the need to dig the way he had. But that was who he was, what he did. He shouldn't care, but he did, maybe because of their brief interlude and the fact that she was living right next door to his family. It seemed the O'Connells attracted only trouble and scandal.

"Oh, I don't know," he said. "What about yesterday at the wedding, where you pretended not to know me? As if we hadn't met…"

"So did you, Luke, so who's really the liar? I changed my name to protect myself, but you pretended to be someone you weren't, and now here you are, in my face, dissecting my life and looking into my background. Is trouble going to land on my doorstep now just because your family wanted to introduce me to you? I should have said no when Jenny and Tessa mentioned it."

"I never said I was a saint, but let's put that weekend aside. I'm sure we can both agree that I lied, but I had reasons, and this is about your situation. My intention isn't to create a problem for you. You should have just come clean and told me."

By the face she made as she sat up straighter, he wondered whether she agreed.

"Convenient, isn't it, Luke, that you've suddenly decided you can dissect my life and call me a liar? Look in the mirror. I've never hurt anyone, but can you say the same? What kind of trouble are you bringing to my doorstep?"

He made himself pull in a breath before he denied he was stirring things up. What had he done? He had dug, and now the system had been triggered. It could be nothing, but it could be something.

"This isn't about me, Chloe. This is about you and the fact that you're in the system, wanted for questioning. When you left Wyoming, did you know the cops wanted to talk to you?" He wondered whether she'd answer.

"I left because I came forward and told them the arsonist was the town's golden boy, Dirk. I saw him while out walking my dog. It was the middle of the day, not late at night. Why he would do that to that family, I don't know. The cops, the sheriff, the deputies all assured me I'd be protected, but as soon as the trial started, things suddenly went sideways for me. I should have known the jury would never convict him. After he was acquitted, there was no protection, and I was a target. The local cops who had given me those assurances turned their backs on me."

She gestured to her chest. A heaviness had settled in the room, a feeling he was too familiar with. "The same cops who'd said they had my back were suddenly looking at me as a problem. My house was broken into when I was at work, and I came home to find the place a mess, with a note that said, 'Leave town if you know what's good for you.' Did I call the cops? Sure, but they took their time, said they'd canvas the neighborhood, basically paid me lip service. They weren't interested in helping me.

"I saw it then, how angry they were, and I realized it was at me. So I didn't bother calling them when my tires were slashed. I didn't call them when Mr. Goldman, a retired old man, called me out in the middle of the grocery store, yelling that I should be ashamed of myself for making up a lie the way I did. He even grabbed my cart and wouldn't let me pass, yelling so everyone could hear as they stood and watched, saying I was a horrible person and I should be the one locked up. I walked out of the store without my groceries.

"Then complaints were filed against me with the town—you know, noise complaints? Bylaw officers showed up, saying my dog was a nuisance, and then animal services drove up with a complaint of animal endangerment. They took my dog, BJ, a little terrier mutt. I started to consider it then, moving. The next day, I went back to work at the toy store I managed, and the owner fired me. Said there were too many complaints about me, that he couldn't risk his business. I went home and cried for a day, and then I realized I had to go.

"So I sold off what I could, which wasn't easy in a town that hates you, and with my savings I bought a ticket to Greece. I stayed there for two weeks. That was where I met you, Henry, and for a moment I didn't have to worry about what was coming at me or about being hated so much, because nobody knew who I was. It was wonderful. But the trip burned through a lot of my savings, so the rest is history. When I left, I was being harassed, but you say the cops now want to talk to me. About what, exactly? Because that's news to me. Then, I didn't leave a forwarding address when I returned from Greece. I just moved here, adopted a new name. And now here you are, trying to destroy what I've built."

As he listened to her talk, he found himself trying to remember that weekend with her, trying to see her as a woman who'd been running. She hid it well. "I'm not trying to destroy anything, Chloe. If this is true, you need to talk to the cops and find out what they want. For you to be flagged could mean something."

She nodded. "I suppose this is where you tell your family. You know, Tessa was trying to get me to apply at the high school. They have an opening for an administrative assistant, a good job. She believes I could do so much better than as a nursery assistant at the gardening store. But at a school, everyone has to have a background check, and mine would come back with a different name. So I told her no over and over. Even Suzanne and Jenny encouraged me, because no one wanted to believe I could be happy with a minimum-wage job, watering plants all day. Now here you are, making calls about me. Do you have any idea how I'm feeling? So no, I think I'll decline talking with anyone from Cody."

She slipped off the stool and strode to where her laptop was plugged in on the counter. She opened it and typed something in, then walked it back over to him so he could see the news article. "Just so we're clear, everything I said was the truth. You can read it here. The one thing I've wondered this entire time is why he did it, why he started that fire, why he burned the house down and killed that family. Yet now I'm seen as the bad guy. Honestly, now I can't blame people for not coming forward when they see things they shouldn't."

He took in the article, her photo splashed on the front page. "I'm sorry," was all he could think to say. He thought of the reason he had come there, to ask her out, yet he'd just learned everything he hadn't expected.

"Should I say thank you? I think I won't." She gestured to the door. "If it's all the same to you, I'd appreciate it if you'd leave, because I'm done talking about this. There. You have what you need, and you'll do what you want with it, but, respectfully, please don't come back." She pulled her arms across her middle.

He could feel the wall between them. He had found out the secret she was hiding, but now he wished he could heal the pain and hurt he had caused. He only nodded as he started walking to the door. His hand on the knob, he glanced back to her. "For what it's worth, I won't say anything. But, Chloe, you should call Marcus and talk to him, at least to find out what these cops want to talk to you about."

She only stared up at him as if he were responsible for all her misery. He took in the heavy curtains and blinds, still closed, not allowing any light in, and he understood a little better why she was shutting out the world.

"Goodbye, Luke," was all she said.

He pulled open the door, seeing the bright sunny day. Yet his brother's sheriff's car was parked out front, and there was Marcus, walking to the door.

"Luke," Marcus said as he stepped onto the front step, though he looked at Chloe right behind him. When he pulled off his sunglasses, Luke realized this wasn't a personal call. Gone was the smiling, teasing family friend. "Okay, this is awkward, but I got a call from Cody, Wyoming," he said. "The sheriff there told me about a person of interest, Chloe Welch. I saw the name of the assumed identity, Misty Bates…" Marcus gestured to her, looking at her with the kind of suspicion that came with being a cop—and all because Luke had gone poking around.

"Well, that didn't take long," she said, staring up at Luke accusingly. "So what is this, Marcus? Luke is here because of the very same thing, but he was asking, checking. You did say that trouble could be coming my way, so evidently, here it is." Her arms were crossed, and he could feel the bite in her words, the accusation.

What could he say? She was absolutely right.

His brother was uncomfortable, judging by the way

he pulled his hand over the back of his neck. "So you were expecting me? Maybe I should ask what this is about, because it seems you're in some trouble. The police in Cody want to talk to you. You want to fill me in?" Marcus rested his hands on his duty belt.

Luke could feel how official this had suddenly become. He wondered whether Chloe had any idea.

"Not particularly," she said. "But let me guess: They're on their way?"

Marcus dragged his gaze from Luke to Chloe. "They want you brought into our office so they can pick you up and bring you back for questioning."

For a moment, he wondered whether Marcus was there to arrest her.

Maybe Chloe was thinking the same thing, as she said, "Am I under arrest, Marcus?"

He shook his head. "Nope. This is more of a request —but I'm wondering now what I should call you. Is it Misty or Chloe?"

Luke took in the redhead behind him, who now seemed so alone.

"Chloe is fine, considering we are way past me having any privacy," she said. "But at the same time, I think I will decline your request."

Marcus's expression was suddenly hard, and Luke could see Chloe was fast getting on his wrong side, yet he said nothing.

"As is your right," Marcus said. "But I have to ask you, why the assumed name? What are you running from? What is this really about?"

He wondered whether Marcus wanted to ask more. He had stopped just short of asking what kind of trouble she was bringing to their family.

"You know what, Marcus?" Luke cut in, taking in the confusion on Marcus's face. "Chloe is not about to answer that, considering there's more going on than you realize. The only reason you're here is because I was poking around and digging. You say the Cody cops are on their way here to talk to Chloe, but you don't know what it's about? I have an idea."

Chloe was staring at him with the oddest of expressions.

"Chloe, I think maybe you should call a lawyer," he continued. "Whatever it is the Cody police want to talk to you about, you should have someone looking out for your interests this time."

She only inclined her head and let out a sigh. "Yeah, I agree," she said. Then she dragged her gaze over to his brother. "Marcus, it seems I should apologize for something, but what, exactly, I'm not sure, because I'm still the same person you knew yesterday."

# CHAPTER
## Seven

Luke took in the office: the dark-haired lady doing Charlotte's old job, Colby doing some paper-work, and Harold talking on the phone, lifting his hand in a wave as Luke walked past him into the sheriff's office behind Marcus. He didn't close the door, just took in his brother as he walked around the desk, rested his hands on the back of the chair, and leaned there as if considering everything.

Marcus looked back over to Luke. "I just don't get this. What is it with our family? It seems we're a magnet for this sort of thing. So the woman I've known, who is friends with my wife and all of us, isn't who we thought she was. Her name isn't Misty but Chloe, and she's running from something. And we were trying to set you up with her. Maybe I should apologize."

Why did his brother seem so off?

"For what, trying to fix me up with a nice girl?" Luke said. "You should know I'm likely responsible for all this."

Still standing behind his desk, Marcus winced. What

would his brother say if he only knew everything he had done, or the fact that yesterday hadn't been the first time he met Chloe? "Dare I ask how you're responsible? You said it at Chloe's, too. I could see how angry she was with you, closing the door on us. I almost expected her to demand that we get out of her yard. So what is this about, and how are you responsible?"

He lifted his hand to his face and pulled it down, wondering how to explain that the first thing he saw was whatever a person was hiding. He just expected the worst. But with Chloe, he wondered whether there was more to the story.

"Oh, I don't know. Because I can't be happy and I needed to prove something was wrong with her, I went digging into her past. I called Jess, and he said ViCAP had flagged her."

"Well, I guess you got your wish." Marcus was standing now, his arms crossed. "You know, this doesn't look good for her, not coming in. The Wyoming sheriff is expecting some cooperation when he comes, so is there a reason I shouldn't be doing just that? You told her to call a lawyer. Really, Luke, what kind of trouble is she in?"

Luke wondered what censored version he should give his brother. "What she told me or what I know for sure?"

Marcus had a way of looking at people when he didn't know what to say. He made a rude noise and gestured toward him, but there was a knock on the open door. Luke turned to see Harold in his deputy uniform.

He strode in. "Marcus, those Wyoming cops are here, wanting to talk with Chloe Welch," he said before closing the door, something Luke hadn't expected. "I'm having a little trouble with this. What am I supposed to tell Suzanne? She's all over Misty, pushing her right in your path, Luke. I know she was planning to call her today, to drop over there. Is Suzanne walking into trouble? You know how your sister is…"

Marcus shut his eyes.

Luke could see they were taking this in a direction he hadn't expected. "Both of you, knock it off," he said. "Marcus hasn't told you this, but it's because of my digging that the cops are here. I knew she was hiding something, but as I was saying to Marcus, it's not what you might think it is. She witnessed something and came forward about it, and it backfired on her. And you should know we've met before."

Now he had their attention. He had never meant to tell anyone that part.

"Before. When, exactly?" Marcus said. "You mean in town, or are you getting at something else, Luke?"

Harold, who was known for his rather calm demeanor, now seemed anything but.

"It's not what you're thinking," Luke said. "I met her after one of my jobs in another country a few years back." He thought of the kiss goodbye, how good she'd felt, and the fact that she'd walked away from him.

No one was saying anything. He felt his face warm.

Marcus didn't pull his gaze, and something in that one look told him his brother might have an idea of the kind of meeting he and Chloe had shared. "Do I dare ask how well you know her or how you met?" he said.

Luke was never one to kiss and tell. He felt as if everything he'd done from the moment he opened his laptop that morning, wondering what the woman he had known as Misty was hiding, had set something in motion. Now he was jamming up a lady who, he was starting to realize, just wanted to be left alone.

"It was personal," he finally said. "Let's just say she was likely as shocked as I was yesterday when she saw me there. Neither of us knew who the other really was."

There was another knock on the door, and Harold pulled it open to reveal two men Luke had never seen before. One was older, with gray hair, and the other was dark haired and round in the middle, both of average height, with badges over their uniform shirts. So these were the cops.

"Sheriff O'Connell, I'm Sheriff Kolter, and this is my deputy. I spoke with you on the phone about Chloe Welch. Where is she, exactly? Your deputy said she's not here."

Marcus was still standing. Luke wondered which of the two men had told Chloe she'd be safe, that they'd watch her back, only to turn on her when everything fell apart.

The sheriff was looking his way. "Who is this?"

"Luke O'Connell. No one of importance," he said, jumping in before Marcus had to explain why his brother was in the middle of what was sounding like a police investigation.

"I went to see Chloe and asked her to come down to the station," Marcus said. "I told her you were on your way here and that you had some questions for her. She refused, which is her right. She's not under arrest or charged—or am I missing something? Because you didn't really elaborate as to the details on the phone."

Sheriff Kolter had a thick mustache. He rested his hand on his duty belt. "She's wanted for questioning in an ongoing investigation. New evidence has surfaced that links her to an arson and quadruple homicide. With all due respect, Sheriff, we expected a little professional courtesy. We weren't asking her to come in. She was to be here so we could take her back to Cody for questioning."

"Is she under arrest? Are you charging her?" Luke cut in, feeling the direction this was headed.

The sheriff gestured to him with frustration. "Who are you, again? Luke O'Connell, is it? You're related?" he said, an accusation.

"Yes, Luke is my brother," Marcus said. "But he's right. Until you have a warrant, you can't come into my county and order me to pick up one of our citizens because you want to talk to her. That's not how things work here. I asked her, and she said no. Pretty sure she's calling a lawyer now, so if you want to talk to her, it's not going to be with me pressuring her to come in here so you can take her all the way back to Cody."

Kolter pulled a folded paper from his pocket and took one step and then another over to Marcus, holding it out to him. "You want formal? Here it is. A warrant for the arrest of Chloe Welch on suspicion of arson and the murder of a family. You want the details about how a husband and wife and their two young children were killed in a house fire started by Chloe Welch? She accused a local hero, and not only was he vindicated, but evidence has surfaced that Ms. Welch had reasons to target him. It's all there, Sheriff. Now, are you going to take us to Ms. Welch, or are you going to interfere?"

Harold had slipped out of the office at some point, but Marcus was reading the warrant, his lips a fine line as he pressed them together and shook his head.

"No, I'll take you," he said. "This is... I don't know

what to say." He dragged his gaze over to Luke, then back to the sheriff and his deputy. "You can follow me over to her place."

Luke watched as the sheriff reached for the warrant. Marcus walked around his desk and handed it to him, and then the sheriff and deputy walked out. His heart was hammering, and he wondered what they had on Chloe.

Marcus stopped right in front of him. "You know she did something?" he said, and Luke wasn't sure whether he was asking or telling him.

"It may not be what you think," Luke said. "She told me she had to leave Cody because she saw a local hero do something and came forward, and now she has a target on her. Is there more? I don't know, Marcus."

His brother let out a sigh. "Sometimes I really hate the secrets people keep."

For a moment, Luke wondered if that was about Chloe or their own family. "You mind if I tag along?"

Marcus said nothing for a second, then inclined his head. "You can ride with me. And maybe you can fill me in on the drive over about what exactly happened and why two Wyoming cops are here with a warrant for a lady who, until this morning, I believed to be someone else."

# *Eight*

Pulling up with Wyoming cops on his brother's quiet street would have the neighbors talking, especially since the cops were now out of their car and walking up to Chloe's door. It was the kind of scene that attracted attention.

Luke hung back only because Marcus had asked him to. There was a time to push and there was a time to listen to his brother.

The knock was loud. "Sheriff's department! Chloe Welch, open up. We have a warrant for your arrest," Marcus called out in a tone that was all business.

Luke remembered something else she'd said, how friends suddenly weren't friends anymore when you were seen as guilty, even before you'd been convicted. He listened to the deadbolt and hadn't expected to see Suzanne on the other side of the door when it opened. She wore a blue maternity top and capris, her long hair pulled back in a ponytail.

"Marcus, what do you want?" She pulled her arms over her chest, resting them on her swelling belly.

"I need you to step out here, Suzanne," Marcus said. "This doesn't concern you."

He could see his little sister becoming stubborn, immovable.

"Yes, I understand Luke is responsible for this little mess," she said. Apparently, she was taking up advocacy for Chloe, yet he wondered how much she knew.

Chloe appeared beside her, her hand on Suzanne's arm. Something about the exchange told him she'd shared enough with Suzanne to bring her up to speed. Luke didn't say anything, because Suzanne was right, to a point.

"I'm right here," Chloe said. "Suzanne, it's fine. Deputy Wayne, Sheriff Kolter, this is more than questions for me. I see this is rather formal. So now you're arresting me—on what charges?" For a moment, she sounded confident.

"Actually, I want to see the warrant." Suzanne held out her hand to demand it.

Luke thought Marcus was going to put his hands on Suzanne and drag her out of there, but that would only backfire on him, as their little sister didn't appear to be going down without a fight. He could see the warrior in her, a woman looking for a cause. Maybe he should be the one to sit her down and have a talk about figuring out better ways to channel her aggression.

The deputy handed the paper over to Suzanne before reaching for Chloe, turning her around, and cuffing her. She was still in her shorts, but at least she had shoes on. As she was led off the step and read her rights, she appeared too calm, as if she had been expecting this.

He heard a car and turned to see a Mercedes pulling

up and parking at an angle in front of Marcus's cruiser. Karen stepped out. Evidently, she and Jack were still in town at her condo, which he knew she refused to sell. She was in heels and a red sundress, and she lifted her sunglasses and rested them on top of her hair, a mix of copper and blond, hanging long and loose. The governor's wife was striding right over to the sheriff, who had stepped in front of Chloe. At least she seemed to be handling it better than he'd expected.

"I'm Karen O'Connell, and I'm Chloe's lawyer," she said. "What is this about? Why is she handcuffed? Marcus?" Karen could pack a punch with her words even though she was short. Something about her told him she wouldn't go down without a fight.

"They have a warrant, Karen," Marcus said. "It's out of my jurisdiction. Don't get in the middle of this."

Luke knew his siblings could be at each other's throats and fighting in a moment. Evidently, Chloe had called both his sisters.

The Wyoming sheriff motioned to Karen. "That's right. We're taking her back to Cody, so you can talk to her there. She's under arrest on suspicion of arson and murder." He took one step and then another toward Karen, holding his hand up to block her from getting closer.

Chloe seemed to know the deputy who was holding her arm, leading her to the Wyoming sheriff's car.

"Misty—shit!" Karen said. "Chloe, I mean. Don't say a word. Don't talk to them at all until I get there. Do you hear me, Sheriff? You do not question my client or talk to her at all. She's asked for a lawyer, so anything you try to coerce from her I will have thrown out."

His sister could be damn demanding. The sheriff

said nothing, only shook his head as he walked to the cruiser where Chloe had been shoved in back.

Karen jogged across the lawn in her heels. "Chloe, I mean it! Say nothing. No matter what they say or do, don't open your mouth. I'll be there as soon as you are. You heard the rights they read to you. You have the right to an attorney and the right to remain silent. Stay that way!"

He couldn't hear what Chloe said, as the deputy closed the door on her. The sheriff was behind the wheel, and Luke watched as what seemed like a scene from a movie played out before him, all because he hadn't been able to let go of his need to dig up info on a woman his family wanted to introduce him to.

Suzanne slapped his arm. "You just can't leave things be, can you?" she snapped. She had walked over to him, and she leveled the fire in her eyes completely on him.

Marcus was still on the front step, reaching for the front door. Luke wasn't sure what he was doing.

"Marcus, you stay out of her house!" Karen yelled.

Suzanne had that stubborn look on her face, and he thought she swore under her breath. "How could you, Luke? You think she deserved this? You just had to dig, and now Misty…" She shut her eyes and touched her forehead. "I mean Chloe. I can't believe what she was forced to do for a little peace. Yes, I know, because after your little shenanigans here, she called me in tears. I called Karen, and by the time I got here, she was beside herself and told me everything. I can't believe what she's been through, coming forward after witnessing a crime, being promised protection, and then having her life turned upside down because the man was acquitted.

Now the spotlight is on her. What do they have on her?"

He realized she was expecting him to answer, but all he did was glance over to Karen, who had pulled the inside door closed and somehow moved Marcus off the step and onto the grass. There was something about the women in his family. They would take anyone on.

"I don't know everything, Suzanne," he said. "I had a feeling she was hiding something. It's just something I see in people, secrets and lies. After some checking, I found out she used to be Chloe Welch, from Wyoming, but she was flagged when I had Jess do some checking in ViCAP, the federal database. So yeah, I guess I am responsible for this. But I'm not kidding, with how fast this happened, they had to have been in their cars and driving here as soon as she was flagged. They were looking for her. So they had a warrant? This has suddenly gone from her being a person of interest to her being arrested. Are they charging her with arson, with murder?"

Karen didn't seem happy with him, either. "They didn't say they were charging her, but they don't have to right away. Look, I've got to go. They have a long ride with her and a lot of opportunity to work her down before I get there." She reached for her sunglasses and took a step.

"You know, when I first met Chloe in Plaka, after the weekend we spent together, I never in a million years expected this…"

"Weekend together?" Suzanne cut him off.

Karen turned, her eyes big. Apparently, Chloe hadn't shared that part of the story. Even Marcus walked over into his line of sight, staring at him long and hard.

"You knew her before yesterday?" Karen said.

Marcus angled his head. Luke felt Suzanne tap his chest hard with the back of her hand.

"Speak. Do not go silent," she said.

"Okay, so she didn't tell you," he said. "Yes, I met Chloe before, in Greece, nearly three years ago. We met, spent a weekend together, and then parted ways. I never expected to see her again."

His siblings just stared at him as if they didn't know who he was. Then Karen made a rude noise and lifted her hand.

"Okay, I don't have time to hear this," she said. "Seriously, Luke? So let me get this straight. You had a weekend of sex with a woman you just met on the other side of the world, and because of that, you decided to dig into her background?" The way she said it had him thinking he had created this entire problem because of his paranoia.

"Well, when you put it like that, you make me sound like an asshole."

Karen slid her glasses on and looked over to Marcus. "You want to explain how I see it? Because I have to go."

Marcus shook his head. "Nope."

Suzanne was staring daggers his way, and Luke realized that she probably needed time to cool down.

"Karen, how about I tag along with you?" he called out and started walking, leaving Suzanne with Marcus.

"How about you don't, Luke?" Karen said, stepping around her husband's Mercedes and pulling open the door.

Luke rested his hand on the roof. "Please, Karen. Look, I may have screwed up here, but I know she didn't do this. I know bad because I work with it for a living. I can help, and I may be able to fill in some holes in this situation while you drive."

He could see she was considering it. Then she dragged her gaze back to him and tapped the door. "I don't have time to argue here. Fine, get in. But I swear, Luke, you'd better have something."

He heard the ding of his phone and pulled it out to see a text from Jess. "I have better than something." He lifted the phone to Karen. "I have my team, who can do some digging to figure out what's really going on."

# *Nine*

"So you're sure the story is true?" Luke said, taking in the "Welcome to Wyoming" sign they passed on the highway. His sister had kept the sheriff's car with Chloe in their line of sight, and he had Jess on speaker because Karen wanted to hear everything. "Just to be clear," he said, "my sister Karen, the governor's wife, is listening in."

"Hi, Jess," Karen called out.

He knew his team leader was likely taking a second to figure out what he could say and what he couldn't.

"So we're clear and all cards are on the table," she continued, "I'm the acting lawyer for Chloe right now, so if there's something you have to share that was obtained in a questionable way, I don't want to know. Got it?"

Luke only stared at his sister, who was looking straight ahead, determined and a scrapper to the end.

"Okay, good to know," Jess said. "And yes, the story is true. You want details, right? Just be prepared. It's not the kind of crime that will leave you sleeping well at night. There's a lot of anger because a family perished in the fire. Anytime a community hears that a child, let alone an entire family, has been killed and signs point to foul play, you have people out for blood.

"Now, from what you told me, the original report says Chloe Welch testified in the trial of Dirk Randall, who was arrested four years ago. The family was Sal and Deanna Miller and their two children, Rosie and Mickey. Chloe was walking her dog in the small community of Cody and spotted Dirk leaving the house. Smoke was spotted shortly after, then a fire.

"When the fire department arrived, the house was fully engulfed, and firefighters couldn't get in to check for the family. It turned into a recovery, which only fueled the anger in the town, with questions about why the family hadn't gotten out. The kids were found downstairs, huddled together. Reports from the arson investigator stated the door downstairs may have been tampered with, so they couldn't get out. Deanna Miller was in the kitchen, and the autopsy report mentions blunt-force trauma to the back of the head. Sal was found on the stairs to the basement, asphyxiated, likely trying to get the door open.

"Dirk was arrested solely on Chloe's statement. His lawyers basically had a heyday with her in court, though, and managed to get anything usable tossed out. Dirk didn't know the Millers, whereas Chloe did. In fact, there was a history of confrontation between them. The Millers accused her of not picking up after her dog, whereas Chloe had called the police on Sal for taking pictures of her getting dressed through her bedroom window. The Millers owned the house Chloe lived in, so Sal denied the allegation, saying he was collecting evidence for the eviction. No charges were laid. The incident report surfaced along with statements the defence apparently gathered from numerous neighbors in the area, stating Chloe was the aggressor.

"The investigators could find no link whatsoever between Dirk and the Millers. He had no relationship with them, nor did he know them in any way. Chloe left town shortly after the trial, when Dirk was acquitted, and his lawyers pointed the finger at her. Seems that was all it took for the residents to turn on her. She may have been promised protection from the cops, but that didn't happen. Her dog was seized after a report of abuse, and there were multiple incidents with Chloe, confrontations with angry residents. She was basically run out of town."

Karen tossed her head from side to side as if working out a kink in her neck. "So is that everything, Jess, or is there more you can't say because I'm not going to want to hear how you got the information?"

The silence that followed had Luke taking the phone off speaker and lifting it to his ear. "You're off speaker," he said, "so tell me what you aren't saying."

Karen took the ramp off the highway, following the sheriff.

"This girl has really stepped into it," Jess said. "It seems she has an axe to grind with Dirk Randall and the Millers. Did she lie and commit perjury? Because what I managed to find out is that unofficially, the Cody department have had Chloe on their radar and have been building a case against her since the moment she left, with motive and opportunity. They know it was arson, and even though everything is circumstantial, if I was there and had been given the information they have, I'd be seeing her as guilty too. Everything is pointing to her. They had history, and not the good kind."

"So you think she's good for it?" He wondered why he had that off feeling again.

"Didn't say that. I said on paper, circumstantially, everything points to her—all too neatly. When a crime of this magnitude happens and fingers start being pointed, it doesn't take much for a lot of people to start coming forward, remembering bad things about someone, true or not. It spreads like wildfire."

The sheriff's car pulled in front of the red brick sheriff's office, and Luke took in the town, a part of Wyoming he thought he'd driven through once. From his first impression, Cody didn't seem like the kind of place where something like this could happen, but then, heinous crimes could happen anywhere.

"So what are you saying, Jess, that people are suddenly coming forward about her, saying she did it and they saw her, or is this something else?"

"My guess is that you should focus on Dirk Randall, because he walked away squeaky clean. Too clean, if you know what I mean. No one is that clean or perfect. He's successful, single, the kind of guy who owns a lot of the town, likely because of the leg up he got. He has a lot of people working for him, it seems. My guess is that as a teenage hero who saved a senator's kid, he had doors opened to get him where he is today.

"Chloe, unfortunately, seems to have pointed the finger at the wrong person. Her past was put on trial, and she was made out to be bad news. It was nothing unusual from the average teen, but Dirk's lawyers knew how to spin it with the right context, shining light on all that questionable stuff. That's how stories suddenly pop up. She left Cody, changed her name, and moved to another state, to your hometown. Smart, but it was still too close to Cody. I can't blame her. On the surface, it looks like she's guilty, a liar, but if you dig and read, it's not as cut and dried as people believe. So there you go, in a nutshell. This is the girl your family is tossing in your path? Don't take this the wrong way, Luke, but it seems your family attracts this."

He only shook his head, knowing he could've said the same, considering Jess was as screwed up as he was, with no family, no wife, and a life that had become all about his team. "Fine, let's not rehash this," he said. "Look, we just pulled up in front of the sheriff's office in Wyoming, and since you volunteered to dig around on this Dirk Randall…"

Jess swore on the other end. "I don't believe I volunteered for anything."

"I'm asking nicely."

Karen turned off the car after parking across the road from the sheriff's office. She dragged her gaze to him, and he could see the questions she had.

"Keep your phone on," was all Jess said before he hung up.

Luke opened the door as his sister stepped out and reached for her big bag in the backseat. As he walked around the back, she closed up the door and clicked the fob to lock it, then reached over and pressed her hand to his chest to stop him.

"I realize you didn't want me to hear all that," she said, "but give me the Coles Notes version of what he said. Also, it would be best if you waited out here."

There she went, going all lawyer on him.

"Seems enough evidence is coming forward about

Chloe," he said. "She had a kind of tense relationship with the murdered family, with reports of disputes. People suddenly didn't like her, whereas the hero she pointed the finger at is squeaky clean."

Karen frowned as she lifted her shades and rested them on top of her head. "So what are you saying, Luke, that she did it? No, I can't believe it. We've known her as Misty for so long, and I can't believe any of this. She seemed so nice."

He hoped she wasn't suddenly believing she was guilty. "Who says she isn't nice? Maybe she got a raw deal. Karen, you surprise me. Out of anyone I know, you're the first to champion those who haven't gotten a fair shake."

His sister opened her mouth to say something, maybe to argue or disagree, but he stepped forward and rested his hand on her shoulder, then gestured to the deputy who was leading Chloe up the stairs to the station, cuffed. Under arrest, held for questioning. This didn't look good.

"Well, I guess I'd better get in there," she said.

"Yeah, okay. But, Karen, you're going to want me in there, too. As you said, there are some things you may not want to hear, and if Chloe is getting the short end of the stick, it's better if I hear firsthand what they have while Jess is digging on the other end."

She started to say something, then evidently changed her mind. "Fine. Just listen, though, and don't interrupt. Oh, and if they ask, you're my investigator. And if you find something damaging…"

"Yeah, yeah, I get it," he said. "You don't want to know."

**CHAPTER**

*Ten*

"So let me get this straight. She's not under arrest," Karen said, getting straight to the point, from where she sat beside Chloe at a table, the deputy on the other side. The sheriff was leaning against the back wall, against the one-way glass, and Luke would've given anything to know who was on the other side.

"Ms. Welch is a person of interest," the deputy said. "If she hadn't been hiding, we wouldn't have had to take such drastic steps. She is detained for now on an out-of-state warrant with the cooperation of your sheriff."

For a moment, Luke wondered whether the man really understood how the law worked.

"So you're saying you had the cooperation of the Livingston sheriff's office?" Karen said. "You admit the warrant wasn't signed by a judge but rather was issued by this office?" She scribbled something on a notepad and took in the warrant she'd demanded to see again, then glanced over to Luke, who was leaning against the wall opposite, watching the sheriff and deputy on what seemed like a fishing expedition.

"Should we get Sheriff O'Connell on the line?" Karen said. "Because I'm wondering whether you told him you had the correct warrant, signed by a judge, considering this is out of your state jurisdiction."

"You mean your brother?" the sheriff said from where he was leaning, his arms crossed, seeming rather calm.

"The very same. You did tell my brother you had the correct warrant? Because this one doesn't get you Ms. Welch. In fact, you were out of your jurisdiction, and I don't think neighboring sheriffs take kindly to being lied to, especially from other law enforcement. They remember, and I remember. Judges don't like that kind of overreach."

Most didn't, anyway, but then, Luke knew some who did the overreaching themselves.

The sheriff pulled in a deep breath and pushed away from the wall. Karen was pushing the right buttons, but they still didn't have a clue what the sheriff had on Chloe.

"Oops, my bad," Sheriff Kolter said, much to Luke's disbelief, but from the expressions on his and the deputy's faces, he could see they were well aware of the lines they'd crossed, considering Chloe was there now in their jurisdiction. Marcus would need to be more careful.

"So what is this, Sheriff, Deputy?" Karen said. "This warrant is…"

"Suspicion of arson and murder. Isn't that right, Choe? Coming forward the way you did and offering Dirk Randall up kind of backfired on you. So what problems did you have with the Millers? They owned the property you lived in, and they wanted you out, and things escalated. I mean, there were a few incidents when we were called in…"

"You were called in by me because Sal Miller was outside my bedroom window, taking pictures of me getting dressed after I climbed out of the shower," Chloe said. "When you showed up, he denied it, of course. If I remember, it was Deputy Simmons who refused to look at the camera, because Sal Miller owned the house and said he was evicting me and needed to take pictures of the outside for evidence."

"Chloe," Karen said, reaching over to touch her arm, a reminder to let her do the talking.

Chloe tucked her short red hair behind her ears, pulling herself together, and Luke realized she was no longer cuffed.

"The report on file says otherwise," the sheriff said. "A warning was given to both of you, and this was a civil matter, so you were to take it up in court. A number of residents have also come forward in the area to say they heard several arguments between you and the Millers. They indicated you were hostile. They wanted you to leave, and you were causing them grief."

"That's not true!"

Again, Karen had to reach over and touch Chloe. Luke could see they were going right for the jugular, discrediting her, and they knew which buttons to push. He'd have given anything to see what they had, or thought they had, and who was saying what.

"Can I see these statements, please, from these so-called residents?" Luke said. "Are they neighbors? Who are they?"

The deputy angled his head and looked back to him, whereas the sheriff said, "We're gathering everything."

Apparently, that was a no.

"Sheriff, unless you're going to show me the evidence you have against my client, I'm going to ask you to release Ms. Welch," Karen said.

They were already shaking their heads. "Nope, sorry. We have enough to detain her for forty-eight hours."

So they were pushing it all the way, planning to lock her up without charging her, and then what? It seemed they were still trying to figure things out, and he wondered what was really going on. This was a game for them, one in which everything was going to line up neatly and point right at her.

"So I guess I don't understand something here," Luke said. "Chloe came forward after seeing Dirk Randall walk out of the Millers' house. There was smoke and a fire. I understand she called the fire department, as well, am I right? Then you promised protection to Chloe, but Randall hired some high-priced lawyers, and suddenly Chloe was on trial. Randall was acquitted, and the residents turned ugly, so now you're looking at Chloe because…?"

Karen scraped her chair back and narrowed her gaze, looking at him long and hard. He knew the look. She wanted all talking on their side to stop.

"Sure, Chloe was believable," the sheriff said, "but as you said, Mr. Randall was acquitted. The DA has even pointed out that Dirk Randall had no connection they could prove to the Millers, yet we know Chloe did. She also has a history of lying."

Where had that come from?

"Lying? Please show me this history," Karen demanded.

"As we said, everything is being compiled. When this

goes to trial, the DA will provide the evidence to you. So, Chloe, tell us, why the kids? Did you break into the house for another confrontation? Did it get out of hand, and you hit Deanna Miller over the head? Then why the fire? Accelerant was found in the kitchen, the stairwell to the basement. The kids had been trapped down there. Sal Miller died trying to get his kids out. This was all because of issues between you and Sal?"

"We're done with the questions here," Karen said. "I already told you Ms. Welch is not talking, and you've shown no proof that she started the fire or that this is anything but a story you've fabricated. I'll remind you that you will not question my client." She pulled out her card and slid it across the table to the deputy. "Are you still refusing to release her?"

The sheriff gestured to the deputy, who stood up, pulling cuffs from his pouch. He walked around the table toward Chloe, who now stood beside Karen.

"Sit tight," Karen said. "I'll get you out. Remember, no matter what they say to you, you do not talk. They have forty-eight hours to charge you, but I'm going to work on getting you out now."

Chloe only nodded as the deputy held her slender arm and led her over to the door, past Luke. After a moment, she looked his way.

"We'll get you out," he said, but she shook her head. By the way she looked at him, he could see how angry she was. At him, maybe. The door opened, and she was escorted out.

Karen lifted her bag and strode his way, then tapped his arm as he stared across the room at the sheriff, his gray hair, his thick mustache. The man believed she was guilty. It was in his expression, the way he stared at her.

"Luke, let's go," was all Karen said.

He followed her out of the room and down the hall, knowing the cells Chloe had been taken to were in back. Karen pushed open the outside door and pulled out her cell phone.

"Hang on a second," Luke said. "Are we expected to just leave her here for forty-eight hours?"

She reached for her sunglasses and slid them on. "Hopefully not. I plan to find a judge who will hear an emergency motion and release her."

"And you think that will work?" He looked down at Karen. She held her cards close in a lot of ways, but now she made a face, looked out to the street, and shrugged.

"Hopefully. But I'm in unfamiliar territory. Remember, Chloe isn't exactly thought of fondly here. If the local judges hold even a little of the animosity I felt in there, she may have to ride out the forty-eight hours." She looked up at him, and he could see she had a lot of questions.

"Well, that's good. You do that. Because in there, they aren't her friends, and their anger and hate could have them creating evidence just to be sure they get the charges to stick. They believe she's good for this. They believe she's guilty."

His sister firmed her lips and pulled in another breath. "Yeah, I really didn't want to hear that."

"Would you rather I tell you everything is going to be okay?"

She only shook her head, then slapped his chest. "Don't be an asshole. At the same time, I need to sit down with Chloe and find out everything about what happened in her own words, no matter how irrelevant."

He took in his sister, then glanced back to the station. Something about all of this wasn't sitting right with him. "Do you by any chance have the address where this arson happened, where Chloe lived?"

Karen only shook her head. "No, I don't, but I don't think it would be that hard to find. What are you doing, Luke?"

He couldn't explain it, but something about all of this just didn't jive. "Retracing," he said, "going back to the beginning. I think while you do what you need to do here, I'll find out where this house is. I wouldn't mind having a look-see, getting the lay of the land. Maybe I'll have a word with a few of the residents. After all, when a stranger comes around asking questions about something that happened a long time ago, you never know what kind of truth he may uncover."

Karen had an odd expression as she started down the steps. "Let me know what you find out," was all she said.

They strode across the street, and she unlocked her car and slipped inside. Luke couldn't shake the feeling that someone was pulling the strings behind this witch hunt for Chloe.

# CHAPTER
## Eleven

"You sure this is the address?" Luke said to the cab driver as he stared at the vacant lot where a house had once been.

"Sure is. You wanted the Millers' place. Everyone knows where that was. Tragic, really. Had the entire town talking for a long time."

He took in a few houses here and there, one boarded up beside the Millers' place and two other vacant lots across the road. It wasn't the kind of neighborhood he could picture Chloe in. "So the empty lot is where the house was before it burned down."

The cab driver was an older man, once dark haired. The car was still idling as Luke slid the cash over the seat to him. The man only looked back to him in the rear-view mirror. "Tore it down. Nothing was ever rebuilt, but then, the land was bought by the TX Group. They were buying up all the houses on that side. Everything's sold there. Word is there are plans to put in a commercial building for shops and restaurants."

There was a lot of land back there at what seemed to be the edge of town, prime real estate.

"So who are the TX Group?"

The old man just shrugged. "No idea, just a company that brings progress. At least they'll do something here. Once the rest of these houses are gone, I suppose they'll pave it and start building, wipe away the memory. No one wants that kind of landmark. This is an older part of town, anyway."

"Thank you," Luke said, realizing that was likely all he knew. He opened the back door and stepped out, taking in the houses on the other side, the kind of old war homes that needed a lot of work. Loud music was coming from one as he walked the street.

He pulled out his phone, spotting the address of the place Chloe had lived. It had a faded red front and an older screened-in porch, and it looked at least a hundred years old, with its chimney, overgrown yard, and front gate hanging on its hinges.

"Can I help you? Are you lost?"

He heard the voice of an old woman and glanced over his shoulder to the house next door. An older lady, short and dark skinned, her hair almost white, was holding a hose and watering a garden of flowers. He took a step and then another, admiring her white picket fence and small yellow house. It seemed a lot of care had gone into her property.

"Hi. Have you lived here long?" he said, lifting his sunglasses off and resting them on top of his head. He walked closer, staying outside the fence. "Luke O'Connell is my name," he continued when she didn't answer.

"Fifty years. Moved here with my husband, but he died ten years ago. You didn't say what you're doing here. I know everyone who lives here on this street, and I don't recognize you. Never seen you before. You know the people who lived there?" She gestured to the faded red house, which needed work and upkeep.

"No, but I did know someone who used to live there. Chloe Welch."

"Oh," was all the woman said, her hose still going as she watered her garden. "So whatever happened to Chloe? Nice girl, quiet. The place has fallen into disrepair since. She always kept it so nice."

He knew neighbors saw everything, yet this one hadn't immediately jumped to tarring and feathering her. "She moved away to another state. So you had no issues with Chloe?"

She shrugged. "No, as I said, she was good. Picked up after her dog, didn't play loud music, was respectful to me. She did, though, have some problems with the young couple that owned the house. They owned a few houses up the street, too. Never understood why someone needs to own that many houses. You only need one to live in! It was the only time I ever heard her get angry with someone—but there was always something about that man that bothered me. The way he walked around, looking down on everyone." The woman was still spraying her flowers.

He found himself looking at the house Chloe had lived in, then across to the empty concrete lot where the Millers' house would have been. "So what happened to the couple who owned the house?"

The woman flicked her gaze up to him and looked over across the street. "Died in a house fire, of all things. No one got out. Shame, really. But at least Chloe didn't have to worry about him harassing her anymore.

Caught him once looking in her windows, her bedroom. I told him to get out of there. He had no business! Told Chloe to keep her curtains closed, too. Some men just do things like that, even with a wife and kids. Bad is bad." She flicked off the spray nozzle and dragged the hose further to another part of the garden. He took in the black mulch, the tulips, the daisies. Her garden was well tended.

"So you know it was arson, the house burning down?"

She only made a face as she kept watering, then looked over to him. "Of course. Chloe saw that young man the town gave a medal to coming out of the house. She went forward. Told her it was a bad idea, because he was well liked. Towns don't like their heroes doing bad things, especially looking like him. But she did. When the fire department was here, she told them who she saw. The police were here, and that sheriff who keeps getting elected, but it never surprised me one moment when the man got off. Chloe moved not long after, right after they took her dog. A complaint, she said. She was in tears."

"She told me it was a neighbor who filed an animal cruelty complaint."

The woman only shook her head. "Garbage! She loved that dog. And if she hadn't been walking that dog when she saw the man run out of that house, she'd still have it. Sometimes it's best not to say anything, not to get involved. If you see her, tell her Bessie says hi." The woman flicked off the spray nozzle and was about to drag the hose back.

"Bessie, I will tell her," Luke said. "Listen, can I ask whether the sheriff or deputies have been out here to ask you about Chloe and the fire? I understand they're investigating again."

She shook her head. "That sheriff would never set foot on my property. He's not welcome here, and he knows it. Now, why are you asking about that? Is something happening? Why are they investigating? Are they going to take another run at that town hero again?"

He wondered whether the woman even watched the news. "No, not Dirk Randall. They're coming after Chloe."

The old woman turned back to him, and she couldn't hide the shock in her expression. "Excuse me, Chloe? Did I hear you right? They're saying Chloe did it?"

He nodded. "Yeah. That's why I asked about the sheriff and deputy, considering they've said they have all kinds of statements from neighbors. Because of the problems between Chloe and Millers, some ongoing dispute, they say she had a motive."

The woman made a rude noise. "Motive, my ass! That girl didn't start that fire. But when I saw that young man hurrying past, getting into that fancy car, and I saw the smoke not long after, I knew he'd get away with it."

He just stared at her. "You saw Dirk Randall coming out of that house?"

She shrugged. "That's what I said, son. I was in the yard, the sun was out, and Chloe was up the street, walking that dog."

Luke could feel his heart hammering. He heard the ding of his phone and wanted to reach for the woman and hug her. "Did Dirk Randall know the Millers?"

"Well, I don't know how well they knew each other, but he'd been there before. Seen him around. Well, this is just a shame and not right." She was shaking her head, rolling up her hose. "It seems men like him get bigger and bigger and can do anything they want, and no one can touch them."

He wasn't sure what she meant by that. "Are we talking about Dirk Randall?"

The woman wiped her hand on her baggy old floral house dress. Her feet were in slippers. "Sure. He owns everything over there now. Seen him here this past week, and last week several times, too, with contractors. They're taking down all those houses. They'll all be gone, and so will this one next to me, too, since he owns it. He got all the property the Millers owned and four others down that way. But it will be a cold day in hell before he gets my house! I told him that, too. He'd rip it down and turn it into a parking lot for a shopping mall. Guess he finally got what he wanted."

He just stared at her. "What do you mean, got what he wanted?"

She only made a face. "His company. Those houses had to go for his shopping mall, and the land behind it for something else."

So that was what she meant by bigger and bigger.

She gestured with her bony finger to her house. "But my house, he can offer me all the money he wants. He won't have it. I won't sell. Told him so just this morning again when he showed up with that sheriff on that side of the fence right where your standing."

So he was coming with backup. "The sheriff came with Dirk Randall when he tried to buy you out? Did they threaten you?"

She leveled him with a hard look in her dark eyes. "I've seen a lot of things in my eighty-two years, and having a white man show up and threaten me, wanting to take something of mine, is nothing new. I said no, and I meant no. You can live in fear or you can stand your ground. My husband bought this house, I raised our kids here, and I will die here, but I will not be chased away."

His phone dinged again. It was Karen. *Where are you? I got a judge and he ordered her release.*

"Would you be willing to do something for Chloe?" Luke said.

Bessie said nothing at first. The way she was staring at him, he wondered whether she'd say no, but she finally said, "And that would be?"

"Come forward and tell the sheriff what you saw. Because right now, Chloe is being set up for the arson and the murder of the Millers."

She glanced away, and he could feel her hesitation. She lifted her hands and stepped back. "I'm sorry, but no. Although I'm standing my ground on the house, coming forward to that sheriff will only put a target on me. As I said before, bad is bad."

# Twelve

His sister was standing outside the sheriff's office as he pulled up in the back of the same cab, the driver of which had picked him up less than five minutes after he called. He stepped out of the cab after handing the man another twenty, still thinking about the old woman who knew so much. It had been a bombshell, really, but she wouldn't stick her neck out even though she thought fondly of Chloe.

He knew there had to be more to that story.

Karen looked up from her phone as he strode over and up the steps, taking a second to get a feel for a place that had seemed to embrace a monster and wouldn't see the truth.

"Well?" was all his sister said in an unusually sharp and demanding tone.

"Well nothing—though I hit the jackpot, so to speak. Talked to an old neighbor of Chloe's who had a lot to share. She not only confirmed Chloe's story, as she saw her walking her dog that day, but she apparently also saw Dirk Randall leaving the Millers' before the fire. She says Randall has been buying up the block, and he paid her a visit, too. But she won't come forward."

Karen was staring at him in a way that made him pity anyone who got on the wrong side of her. She reminded him so much of a pit bull when cornered. "I can make her," she started, but he only shook his head.

"No, not like this. She'll only dig her heels in. Whatever her reasons, we need to figure those out first. Where is Chloe? You texted that you got her out."

Karen nodded. "You know how many judges wouldn't hear this? Then it just so happened that one did, and I can't say for sure why, but he actually followed the law. He signed the order, and I hand delivered it to the sheriff here. He didn't look too happy. Jack called for an update, and I just stepped outside to fill him in as I waited for you. I guarantee you right now that sheriff is inside, pulling every stop to overturn Judge Roberts's order."

"How do you figure that?"

Karen lifted her unsmiling blue eyes. "Oh, just by the fact that the DA walked in five minutes before you pulled up, while I was talking to Jack. They're likely trying to figure out a way to keep her here. I don't know, but this isn't sitting right. I've got the kind of feeling I've had too many times before when someone is getting screwed over. They're going to charge her, and then I'm going to have to work on bail, because this is just how my day is going." As she spoke, he could hear her frustration. "So who is this neighbor who can help?" she continued. "And why is it that you think my pushing or talking to her will backfire? Because that's what it sounds like you're saying."

The door of the sheriff's office opened, and he saw

her short red hair first, her jean shorts, the old sneakers she had on.

"I don't know what you did, Karen, but thank you," Chloe said after dragging her gaze from Luke. He could feel the tension, the anger. Right, he was responsible for this.

"The warrant wasn't lawful," Karen said. "Let's go for a drive, and we can talk on the way."

The sun was sinking lower. As they turned to leave, the sheriff and another man who looked like a lawyer stepped out behind Chloe.

"So you got a get-out-of-jail pass," the sheriff said. "Don't celebrate too long. It's only temporary, as I expect to have you formally charged again shortly."

The DA put a hand out to stop him from saying more. "Ms. O'Connell, I'm District Attorney Patrick Grisby. As the sheriff was about to say, your client is free for now, but we'd ask that she not leave town, as we have questions, and she is a person of interest."

Karen said nothing. Luke took in the district attorney, who was of medium height and build, in a deep blue suit. He didn't appear any older than Karen.

"We've told Ms. Welch that she is not to leave town," the sheriff said. "We'll consider her doing so to be fleeing the area, which will constitute grounds for a bench warrant for her arrest."

Chloe was only shaking her head, her expression revealing how pissed off she was, yet she was restraining herself better than he would have.

"I'm not clear on why you're telling her she can't leave town," Luke said. "Your arrest wasn't valid. There were no charges, and for that matter, she doesn't live here—"

"Luke," Karen said, cutting him off quite sharply. She turned to the sheriff. "We've extended more than leniency toward you. You haven't charged Ms. Welch, haven't produced any evidence other than hearsay and a story. We're leaving, and right now, we're considering bringing down a lawsuit for overreach on this department, this office, that will have taxpayers on the hook for millions. You want to keep going here? Because I'm done. We're done. If you want to talk to my client again, you do it through me. Chloe, let's go."

Karen was so matter of fact, and Luke took that as his cue. He lifted his hand and gestured for Chloe, who started down, Karen behind her. Luke took a step in the path of the sheriff when he went to follow. He had to look up to him.

"Are we going to have a problem here?" the sheriff said, not stepping back.

As Luke lifted his gaze to him, he could see he was just looking for a reason to pounce. "No problem here. As my sister said, we're done. But let me ask you something, Sheriff. When did you start being a paid thug for a landowner trying to buy up property? Seems to me as if you're confused on your duties. Or is it that the sheriff's office here in Cody, Wyoming, decides what falls under the law?"

For a second, he didn't think the sheriff would answer. He could feel that the DA was staring long and hard at him.

"You accusing me of something, of being dishonest, of corruption? I think you'd better come right out and say what it is you're talking about," the sheriff said sharply.

"Luke!" Karen called out to him, but he didn't look over to her, because he wasn't about to blink first.

"I think you know, Sheriff, what I'm talking about. Why is it that someone who's trying to buy someone else's property gets a police escort? Maybe you threw in some intimidation…"

The sheriff chuckled under his breath. "Oh, I see. This is about Bessie Armstrong. Yeah, well, I'll have you know I only tag along if there's going to be trouble, to keep the peace. Let's be clear: Ms. Armstrong isn't known for her cooperation."

"Luke, come on. Let's go," Karen called out again.

He glanced over his shoulder to his sister, taking in the way she gestured, feisty, ready to storm back over to him and drag him away. Except he wasn't done there, considering he had so many questions about the sheriff and what he was really up to.

He glanced back to him. "And what is that supposed to mean? She's an old woman against two strong men. What exactly do you mean by 'cooperation'? Is it that she won't sell? It's her house, her property. Last I looked, in the US, you can't force someone to sell."

"If it's ordered by the state, we can," the sheriff said.

The DA had said nothing, and Luke wondered whether he had an idea of what was going on.

"You're not talking about eminent domain," he said.

The sheriff rested his hands on his duty belt. "If the government wants your land, they get it. She's been offered fair value, and that's all she'll get. You know how it works. You can't stand in the way of progress, and development means progress. The mall is a big development that will provide jobs."

"A shopping mall, really? And the state has authorized this?"

"I don't have to explain to you how it works. The government wants your land, your property, they can take it, and you have no recourse. The courts always defer to the government. They want the land, and Bessie Armstrong is the only one who's refused to sell. Demolition will start around her. I've already tried explaining to her that she can't stand in the way of progress, that this is for the greater good of the community…"

"You mean it's about driving property taxes up for everyone and lining the pockets of Dirk Randall, making him richer."

The sheriff didn't pull his gaze, but his cheek twitched. Luke was starting to get a better idea of how this puzzle was falling into place.

"Luke!" Karen called again.

This time, he turned away and started down the steps, walking to his sister, seeing that Chloe was already in the back seat. When he looked back to the sheriff's office, all he saw was the door swinging closed as the sheriff and DA walked back inside.

"Seriously, what was that about?" Karen snapped, fire sparking from her blue eyes as she stood in the open driver's door.

He walked around and pulled open the passenger side. "I'm starting to get a better idea of what's really going on."

His sister said nothing, then gestured for him to continue from where her hand rested on top of the car.

He shook his head. "Get in. I'll fill you in as you drive. Whatever it is, it seems all my poking around has done is open a can of worms. We're being pointed in the direction of the age-old basis of every fight, the reason every war has started."

His sister appeared confused. "Huh?"

He tilted his head. "Land, dear sister. It always comes down to land. When someone wants something and someone stands in the way, things can escalate and turn ugly, and that's when someone gets killed. Power, greed, and money. By no means are these people beyond killing a family."

# Thirteen

He'd been watching Chloe in the rear-view mirror, and she paled as they drove toward the state line, with safety waiting on the other side.

"Bessie is a nice old woman, and she did tell me not to go forward," she said. " She told me to keep my head down and ignore it, but I just figured it was because of some of the things that have happened to her. I saw her treated with indignity too many times to count. I wonder if she even saw it."

"So why didn't you say from the beginning that someone else saw Dirk walking out of that house? It seems you were ready to take the bullet alone." He turned in the passenger seat, hearing the leather swish under him. Karen gripped the steering wheel, listening to the back and forth.

"I asked her, and she said no. There was a time to push, but I couldn't make her step up even when I got the shit kicked out of me in court. I made the choice. I made the call…" She shrugged.

Was she thinking of what might have happened, if only? He would have been.

"Even after he was acquitted, she just shook her head and said something I'll never forget: 'You really believed he'd be convicted?' It was like a slap in the face, and one of the last times I saw her outside. My dog was taken the next day…" She lifted her hand, looking out the side window rather than at him.

"I'll get one of our investigators to talk to her," Karen said. "I know one who may be able to convince her."

Luke knew she was talking about the pricey law firm owned by her husband, which he'd stepped away from but she was now part of. He wondered whether she understood what she was dealing with in Bessie.

"I can't afford him or you, for that matter, Karen," Chloe said. "I know the price of your law firm and the hourly rate. I'll be working overtime for the next year to pay the bill…"

He could see that hit a nerve by the way Karen gripped the wheel a little harder.

"This isn't through Jack's firm," she said. "Don't worry about the billing rate and the affordability. Let's just get you out of this jam first, and then we'll talk about what you owe."

Chloe pulled her gaze from the side window where she was sitting behind Karen and stared at the back of her head. He wasn't sure what she was thinking, but he had a pretty good idea of the favor Karen was doing her.

"Your dog…BJ, you said his name was?" Luke said. "You know what happened to him?"

He'd once seen such teasing in Chloe's amber eyes,

but now there was such sadness. The subject of her dog was still an open wound, he could see, from the lump she tried to swallow past.

"He was adopted out to a family. I called that shelter I don't know how many times. I even stopped giving my name, pretended to be someone wanting to adopt BJ, only to be told he'd found a home and a family was picking him up. The girl even said which day it would happen, that afternoon, so I parked out on the road and just waited for hours, then watched as this middle-aged couple with three kids walked him out and put him in a crate in the back of a pickup. I followed them home and waited. You know, I don't know how long I sat there, wondering how long it would be. If they left him outside, I would slip in and take him, and they'd never know. But the hour grew late, and when I saw the joy and excitement on the kids' faces when they took BJ out for a walk, I could see he wasn't in a bad place. Even though he was mine, I drove away and left him, and it damn near killed me."

She didn't say anything else. He knew it was not long after that he'd met her in Plaka. He couldn't make himself say he was sorry even though that was what he wanted to say. *Sorry for everyone who hurt you.*

Instead, he pulled in a breath and let it out a little roughly. "Chloe, you have any idea why Bessie wouldn't come forward? What issues does she have with the sheriff? She have a run-in with him or something? Because she didn't even try to hide her dislike for the man."

She made a face. For a second, her dimples popped with amusement he was positive was at the sheriff's expense. "She has every right. When I came forward, I saw a different sheriff from the one Bessie knew and spoke of, because I had friendliness and supportiveness, the assurance they would see to it that I was protected. I was almost convinced she'd just gotten off on the wrong foot with them. But I was wrong. As soon as I wasn't seen as credible, they turned on me.

"For a moment, I thought she'd say, 'See? I told you.' She'd told me what happened to her husband. He ran a ranch just west of here, and someone left the gate open. One of the bulls got out and rammed a vehicle, then was injured by another car. Her husband was called and went out there, and all she said was that he loaded up his shotgun, muttering that the deputies would only make matters worse.

"Her husband never came home. The sheriff showed up, said there was gunfire and his deputy had shot and killed her husband. The deputy was never charged. Instead, it was called a confusing situation, with the bull and the gunfire. He ruled it an accident. Only two witnesses said there had been an argument. The two deputies wouldn't put that injured bull down, so Bessie's husband pulled out his rifle to do the job.

"One of the deputies yelled at him and shot him. He was dead before he hit the ground. You hear about it happening and think it's sad, and you wonder what was going through the minds of the deputies. But the sheriff wasn't willing to get any justice for Bessie's husband. It was his old boys' club, and she knew it. So does that answer your question?"

He hadn't expected that, but it gave him a clearer idea of the mindset of the sheriff and why Bessie hated him. "It helps. Also confirms why she doesn't trust him. Can't say I do, either. Did you know Dirk Randall is buying up all the property in that neighborhood? He owns just about all the houses in the area now. Apparently, Bessie is the last holdout, and the sheriff showed up with Dirk this morning, bright and early, but she's digging her heels in. The sheriff said the state is using eminent domain. Whoever Dirk Randall is, he's got the power of Wyoming behind him, because they're stating it's in the public interest that Bessie sell her house—for progress, for jobs, even though it'll be another shopping mall we don't need."

Chloe only shook her head. Karen was shaking hers, too, before she pressed the phone button on her steering wheel and said, "Call Jack."

He heard the ring, the click.

"Are you on your way back tonight?" Jack said.

"Yes and no. I'm just leaving Cody, heading back to Livingston. I'll likely stay in the condo tonight. We have Chloe with us. Luke found out something about Wyoming citing eminent domain to take land for a big development. Can you check into what that's about? I mean, you're friends with the Wyoming governor, right? What's his name?"

There was silence for a moment. Luke could almost picture Jack shaking his head and maybe thinking of all the ways to tell her no.

"You know very well it's Lisa Kissinger, first woman they voted in," he finally said.

Karen only nodded. "Sure, okay. So call her and ask her what the hell she's doing with Dirk Randall, buying out some neighborhood for a shopping mall…"

"There's the property behind it, too, a lot of land," Luke cut in. "Find out whether Randall is part of the TX Group and what his role in the company is. Heard their name tossed out."

"You do realize you're asking me to interfere in another state's business…"

"Jack, call this woman," Karen said. "And you're not interfering; you're just asking for information. If the state is upholding some eminent domain policy to seize land, this should be public information."

Jack groaned on the other end. "Why do I feel you're going to ask for more?"

"Thanks, darling. I love you." Karen gave a kiss in the air, then pressed the button to disconnect.

Luke took in the highway, the sign for the Montana state line just up ahead, and he wondered whether that was why he heard Chloe let out a sigh that sounded too much like relief.

Then he heard the blast of a siren. He turned to look out the back window, seeing the flashing lights as the siren blasted again.

"Shit," Karen said. She flicked on her signal to pull to the side of the road.

"No, keep driving and pull over past the state line," Luke said, gesturing straight ahead.

"Luke, there's a cop behind me. I have to pull over," she said, but she kept her foot on the gas.

"Pull over," he heard the loudspeaker blasting out. Then a second cop car appeared and sped around her, moving in front of her, deliberately slowing her and forcing her to the side of the road. The "Welcome to Montana" sign was ten feet in front of them.

"Now what?" Karen said as she put the car in park.

One car was behind them, one in front, angling them off the road. He spotted Sheriff Kolter emerging from the car in front, walking their way. He tapped on Karen's window, and she rolled it down.

"What is this about, Sheriff?" she said.

"Step out of the car, all of you," Kolter said, then pulled open Karen's door. The deputy appeared and opened the back door, reached in, and pulled Chloe out. "Chloe Welch, we have a warrant for your arrest."

*Here we go again,* was all Luke could think as he opened his door and stepped out.

Chloe was cuffed again, along with Karen. As he heard the sheriff reading his sister her rights, citing failure to stop, he knew the man had no idea who Karen was married to. The car was still running, and Karen was stuffed in the back seat of the sheriff's car, Chloe in the deputy's.

Luke started around the car and heard his phone ding, but he didn't pull it out. As the sheriff started back to him, Luke just lifted his hands. "So is this where you arrest me, too?"

The sheriff laughed. "If I could find a reason, I would," he said as he stopped right in front of him, unsmiling. Did the sheriff expect him to lose it, to do something? The man had no idea that Luke dealt with the kind of people who would eat him for breakfast.

Luke only lifted his hands and shook his head. "Tell me the charges against Chloe and my sister. You know Karen will be out by the time you get her back to the station."

The sheriff shook his head. "Maybe, maybe not, but failing to stop is serious, even for a lawyer. And as for Chloe, this time we're officially charging her with arson and murder."

The sheriff nodded and stepped back, and as the deputy pulled away, all Luke could think was that somehow, they had found the final nail in Chloe's coffin. He listened to Karen's Mercedes still running as the sheriff walked back to his cruiser and gave him a mock salute before sliding behind the wheel and pulling away.

He was too confident, and that was something Luke didn't like. Whatever it was the sheriff had dug up or manufactured, he'd bet anything it would be solid and ironclad. Chloe really had stepped on the wrong toes. Now more than ever, he was determined to find out what Dirk Randall was mixed up in, who he was connected with, and what his business was really about.

# Fourteen

"It took you long enough," Luke said, having synced the Bluetooth of his cell phone to Karen's Mercedes. He was behind the wheel and pulling a U-turn, gunning the engine to catch up with the sheriff and follow the cars back to Cody. For the second time today, the sheriff was hell bent on seeing to it that Chloe went down for something he was convinced the man himself had a hand in.

"It takes as long as it does. You know that," Jess drawled in that way of his. "Do you want to know what I found out or not? And where are you, exactly, anyway?"

"Funny you should ask. It seems I'm suddenly in a game of cat and mouse, the kind of shitshow I don't like. Karen managed to get a Judge Roberts to sign off on releasing Chloe, and we were almost at the Montana border when they caught up with us. Needless to say, they have Chloe again and are officially charging her with arson and murder. Karen, too…"

"They arrested your sister?" Jess cut in, his tone

incredulous. "They arrested the wife of the Montana governor?" He laughed.

Luke would have laughed too if the situation weren't so dire. "Yeah, considering she uses her maiden name, they have no idea."

"Wouldn't want to be them when they figure it out," Jess said. "Okay, so here it is. You asked me to dig around on Dirk Randall, major shareholder in a company called the TX Group—a developer, among other things. It's a publicly traded company that has made billions for its shareholders. He funds a local Special Olympics in Wyoming and attends every big competition, so he's kind of a big deal with that, and he's funded some local campaign to help out the under-privileged in the area, too, so he's well known. His public image is squeaky clean, but his company picked up the properties within two blocks of the Millers' burned-down home, including the other houses the Millers owned. They bought them from the estate…"

"Yeah, that part I know already. He's putting in some shopping mall, but there's one uncooperating homeowner. Randall managed to get the state to invoke eminent domain. Someone must really want this devel-opment to go through."

"So you've been busy," Jess said. "But did you know the governor was approached twice by TX? The first time, she refused, but the second, they highlighted the jobs they would be bringing to a distressed area. The land across the road will be a major shipping facility for one of the big box stores across to the west coast. With the deal they worked out, TX is not really putting up the money for the land. In the end, it will be the taxpayers who foot the bill, and TX will get years of tax breaks.

The company has done the same thing in four other states, in distressed areas. They're getting bigger, and when they're that big, the governor isn't as willing to say no. I figure she was boxed in, and TX likely pointed out to her that her saying no would be political suicide, because turning away jobs is frowned upon by the voting public."

Luke only shook his head. He heard a beep and saw Jack's name on the screen. "Look, Jack's calling on the other line. Find out something else for me, would you? Dig around on the sheriff here. I don't know. There's just something about this guy that isn't sitting right with me." The phone beeped again. "I've got to go. Just tell me about anything you find."

"Okay, will do," Jess said. "Luke, sounds like this may be the kind of place you want to be extra careful." Then he hung up.

Luke pressed the green answer button. "I suppose you're probably wondering why your wife isn't answering her phone."

"Yeah. So why isn't she?" Jack said in a way that made it clear he was not happy about any of this or the position Karen was putting him in. "Put her on the phone," he demanded. There was the Jack they knew and loved.

Luke only shook his head, keeping the sheriff's car two car-lengths in front of him. "Can't. She's currently under arrest and cuffed in the back of the sheriff's car, charged with failing to stop or some bullshit like that. Chloe is under arrest, too, now formally charged with arson and murder, in the back of the deputy's car. I'm following both in your Mercedes—which really drives like a dream…"

"Excuse me? What the fuck are you talking about, Luke?" Jack cut in, his voice low and quiet, on edge, likely trying to wrap his head around what he'd said. "Karen is arrested for failing to stop for a police officer, seriously? Does this asshole not know who I am, who she is? Did she seriously do that? What the hell are you two doing? You were supposed to be going to Cody to get that friend of the family out. I still can't believe this mess."

Luke couldn't fight the twitch of his lips even though the situation was completely dire in some ways. "You know Karen doesn't use your name. She's an independent attorney, Karen O'Connell, and I guarantee you the sheriff doesn't have any idea who she's married to. Already warned him she'd be out by the time she arrives at the station. In case you're wondering, we were almost at the state line. She didn't run, though I asked her to. The sheriff cut her off and forced her to stop. He's likely trying to spin it."

He thought Jack swore.

"Oh, and I already heard back from someone on my team, in case you were calling Karen about the TX Group. Dirk Randall is part of the company, and they have their hands in some major developments, some shipping facility for one of the big box giants. Apparently, the governor felt she had no choice."

"Pretty much what she told me," Jack said. "The area was full of distressed homes at the edge of town, right in a prime location for a commercial property. They needed it to be right there because there's no other place with the kind of access they apparently need. She has no choice, even though it will drive up property values and taxes and provide low-paying jobs that will displace the workers, who will have to move further out because they won't be able to afford living there. It's vicious, but it's legal. Okay, time to end this bullshit," was all Jack said.

Luke could feel his sister's husband's anger through the phone. "I take it you're calling the sheriff, and Karen will be waiting when I pull up?" He knew he shouldn't let his sarcasm come through the way it was, but he just couldn't resist. He intended to be right there when the sheriff found out how badly he'd screwed up.

"Oh, I'll be doing more than that. Sit tight," Jack said before he hung up.

Luke settled in for the drive. Twilight was edging in, and the growl in his stomach told him it had been a long time since breakfast. Maybe by the time he got his sister out, they could figure out plan B from a local diner, because as he figured it, Chloe would be spending the night in the most uncomfortable of accommodations.

There was something about the young lady he'd met on the other side of the world over three years earlier. The pieces were starting to fall together.

All this because she'd been doing the right thing.

Then there was Bessie, the old neighbor who wouldn't stick her neck out. He considered for a moment, as he drove, what it would take to get her to come forward. Her husband had been killed. Sometimes, he thought, getting justice was the only thing a person wanted.

Darkness had settled in just as they approached Cody, and Luke flicked on his headlights and parked in the same spot across the street by the center of the town, just down from the sheriff's office, keeping both eyes on the cruisers parked in front of the station.

He heard the ding of his cell phone and saw texts from Marcus, Suzanne, and an unknown blocked number, which he knew was his dad, with the kind of cryptic message he was familiar with. He stepped out of the car as Karen and Chloe were led into the station, cuffed like common criminals.

When his phone rang and he answered, he was met by his father's deep voice.

"Tell me you have a handle on this," Raymond said.

Yup, he had evidently followed along after his last call, his last message.

Marcus and Ryan would likely have taken issue with him calling their dad first, but he knew his dad understood the dark side of politics and state business better than anyone. Having to explain less was better.

"Karen and Chloe have just been taken into the sheriff's office, likely to be booked. I expect Karen will not be sitting in a cell when I get inside, though. I'm sure Jack has already made some calls, and heads are going to roll among those who put their hands on his wife."

He could hear the whir of a helicopter. The way the blades cut through the air, he was having a hard time hearing what his dad was saying. He looked up to see the flashing lights hovering overhead, and he had his hand up as the wind whipped around him.

It was just over him, lowering to the open park, and he spotted another car pulling up in front of the sheriff's office. Sure enough, there was the DA, who glanced over before jogging inside.

"Dad, listen. Can you call Marcus and Suzanne, fill them in? As soon as I know more, I'll call, but I think the cavalry is about to arrive. Jack's here," he shouted into the phone, seeing the Montana logo on the chopper as it landed.

He stayed where he was after he hung up, unable to hear what his dad had said. He closed the door of his sister's fancy car and lifted his gaze to see Montana state troopers and Jack stepping out of the helicopter, the blades still whirring, cutting through the air with the kind of booming that went right through him. The lights flickered.

He was torn for a moment between standing there and waiting for his brother-in-law or seeing the face of the sheriff before Jack walked in.

Jack was already walking right his way, evidently

having spotted him, so he took one step and then another toward him, hearing the chopper winding down, waiting for the governor to raise the hell he needed to.

"Quite the entrance," was all he said as Jack approached in a dark suit and tie, flanked by the state troopers. He was all business in each step, unsmiling.

"Well, I didn't have hours to sit in a car and drive out here. Where's Karen?"

Luke only gestured to the small-town sheriff's office and started walking with Jack, who was shorter than him but took each step in a way that said he could make anything happen. When he asked, everyone acted. "You know, Karen is really going to dig in now…" Luke said.

"Well, so am I," Jack cut in rather sharply, pissed off, ready to go to battle. "I spoke with Lisa Kissinger, the governor here, and I expect she'll have already ordered my wife's release. But she wasn't too happy with my interference in state issues, as she called it, or my questions abut the TX Group and Dirk Randall. She especially didn't like my rather blunt accusation that the sheriff has had a role in ensuring this development deal goes through. This dirty business is now touching my family, so I made it clear to Lisa that she needs to end this bullshit and rein in that company, because the sheriff went one step too far when he arrested my wife."

He wasn't sure what Jack had done, but he knew these kinds of politicians didn't like negative press. One of the troopers pulled open the door, and the other walked in first, ahead of Jack. There were the sheriff and the DA, whose faces said it all. They hadn't expected this kind of shitstorm. By the way Sheriff

Kolter was looking at Jack and then at him, he could tell the man had no idea whose toes he'd stepped on.

"Governor Curtis, I'm sorry," the DA said. "I was just telling Sheriff Kolter about—"

"You arrested my wife," Jack said, cutting off the DA before he could finish his long-winded explanation or say it had been a simple mistake, "on trumped-up charges, so don't start in about how you didn't know she was the wife of the Montana governor, because your overreach will not go unnoticed." Jack didn't stop until he was right in front of the DA and the sheriff.

"I can assure you the charges were justified."

Luke wanted to shake his head at the way the sheriff was seriously considering butting heads with Jack. Evidently, he didn't understand who Jack Curtis was.

"Really?" Jack said. "And the dashcam footage will support that, or did you, in fact, dangerously run my wife off the road when she was trying to safely pull over? You've flagrantly targeted a private citizen of my state, Chloe Welch, and produced a warrant issued by this office with no legal basis, then arrested her and transported her across state lines, even going so far as to lie to a county sheriff in another state that you had genuine authority! You know which warrant you need for this, and what you produced violates all of that. You're setting a dangerous precedent where jurisdictional authorities cannot trust outside law enforcement. If we really want to get into legalities, what you did is called kidnapping, which becomes a federal crime. Where is my wife?" Jack dragged his gaze accusingly from the sheriff to the DA and back. "I expect her to be released in the next thirty seconds, or…"

"She's already released. One of the deputies is

bringing her up," the DA said, motioning with both hands as if to calm a wild animal. Maybe he'd figured out how badly this could go and was already doing damage control. "It was a mistake, is all. She is free to go. Our apologies again, because it was simply a misunderstanding by the sheriff, considering tensions have run high with this case. Isn't that right, Sheriff?"

But Luke could see the sheriff wasn't about to fall in line willingly. He suspected the man had likely had no more than a few seconds' warning and was still trying to wrap his head around what he'd stepped into, then figure out his next step before the entire farce blew up in his face.

"Sure," was all the sheriff said, gesturing toward Jack, though his tone said he was pissed off. The phone was ringing in the background.

"Sheriff, the governor is on the phone for you again," said a young man in a deputy's uniform from a desk in the corner, holding out the phone.

The sheriff let out a rough breath and reached for it. "Yes, Governor?" was all he got out.

Luke pulled his arms over his chest, his stomach rumbling again.

The sheriff turned away, nodding, apparently getting an earful. "I understand, yes…"

Jack and the DA had stepped away, and he spotted Karen walking up, her hair a mess, one of the deputies behind her. Jack was already heading over to her, whereas the DA lifted his hand to his face and pulled it down as if he was having a really bad day.

The sheriff hung up the phone and said to the deputy, "Go get Ms. Welch."

Karen was furious, shaking her head at whatever

Jack was saying to her. "I want to see all the evidence you have in the case against my client, Chloe Welch," she snapped at the DA. "You think I'm going to just take that bullshit move by your sheriff and deputies? You've dropped the charges against me because my husband is the governor and you realized you pulled your trumped-up charges on the wrong person, someone you can't get away with harassing…"

"I understand you're upset," the DA said, cutting her off.

Karen stalked over to him. Spitting mad was an understatement, and Luke was fine with leaning against the empty desk and staying out of his sister's way. Jack was staring at his wife as if he hadn't figured out how to get her to dial it back. This was Karen, after all. Going quietly into that night was something she would never do.

"Upset? Your sheriff cut me off on the highway, dragged me out of the car just before we crossed the state line, and cuffed me, charging me with some bull-shit. My signal light was on to pull over. Even this entire case against Ms. Welch is completely circumstantial. Why the spin? We already know Dirk Randall, your local hero, has been strongarming residents into selling their properties, showing up with the sheriff to make sure he can demolish a city block for—"

"Progress, I think, is what you mean to say," the DA jumped in. The sheriff was now gone, to where Luke didn't know, though he'd have given anything to know what the governor had said to him.

"Is that what you're calling it?"

"Mrs. Curtis, with all due respect…"

"It's O'Connell," Karen snapped.

Jack strode over to her, sliding off his suit jacket and slipping it over her shoulders, his hand on her back.

"As I was saying," the DA said, "the TX Group will get their land deal, as it's what's good for the economy, for the town. We apologize for the misunderstanding. I've been informed the charges against Ms. Welch have been dropped. As you've said, the case is circumstantial."

The sheriff was walking out with Chloe, who was still in her shorts, running her fingers through her short red hair. Whatever the sheriff said to her, she didn't look pleased.

Karen strode directly to her, and Jack took the few steps over to Luke, pulling his hand over his face, his white dress shirt neat and tidy. The Montana state troopers remained close.

"You care to share what the governor said to the sheriff?" Luke said.

Jack glanced over his shoulder, and Luke just watched as the DA made his way down the hall, following the sheriff. Maybe the two needed to get on the same page as to what the orders were. He knew well when someone's wings were being clipped. This investigation had just been closed.

"Oh, likely to turn the spotlight away from Chloe Welch. A family died in a tragic fire, and right now Cody needs all of this to go away. So the case is going to be filed away as ongoing, because this development, according to the governor, has already got the state taxpayers on the hook."

"So Dirk Randall walks free," Luke said.

Jack didn't pull his gaze. "Dirk Randall was acquitted by a jury of his peers. He cannot be recharged, even with new evidence. You know this. It's called double jeopardy."

Luke only nodded.

"But keep in mind that doesn't mean he can't be charged with something else," Jack said.

"Is that your way of saying we could soon hear something about justice coming for this local hero?"

Jack gestured to Karen and Chloe, who were walking their way. "Let's just say that sometimes, playing the long game and waiting pays off. If he committed one crime as heinous as this, there will be something else. But if it's all the same to you, Luke, I'd like to get out of here. I have an early meeting and would like to get my wife home. And one more thing. That girl over there, the one your family was trying to set you up with? How about just asking her out? Stop trying to dig up reasons why you can't be happy." Jack slapped his arm before turning to say something to the troopers.

Chloe walked over to him with Karen.

"Are you okay driving my car with Chloe?" Karen said. "Seems Jack is insisting I ride back in the state helicopter."

Jack hovered behind Karen. Luke was surprised she was giving in.

"Yeah, go with your husband," he said. "I'll drive your car and Chloe home. We'll talk tomorrow."

Karen pulled in a breath and glanced over to Chloe, who was beside her.

"Go," Chloe said. "I'm fine, Karen, and thank you again for getting me out of this jam."

He could see how tired she was as she hugged Karen, who stepped back and, holding Jack's hand, walked out of the sheriff's office.

Luke gestured for Chloe to follow as he held the door, then stepped out behind her, pulling Karen's Mercedes keys from his pocket.

"So is it true they won't be showing up on my doorstep again to arrest me for the Millers?" Chloe said.

He wanted to reach over and touch her as they strode across the street, side by side. His sister and her husband had climbed into the helicopter, which the pilot had already started, the blades cutting through the air, noisy. The wind stirred and had him putting his hand on Chloe's back, her shoulder, as they walked around the Mercedes to the passenger door. He pulled it open, but he waited until the helicopter lifted off and he could hear himself think.

"They won't be coming after you," he said. "Sounds like the governor ordered the case closed."

"So Dirk gets away with it."

The helicopter was now in the distance, the lights flickering and flashing in the darkened sky. He was reminded of the promise he'd made to his mom.

"Dirk Randall was acquitted," he said. "It's the way our legal system works. He can't be recharged. But you don't need to hide anymore. I'm wondering if you'll have dinner with me."

She stared up at him with an odd look on her face. "Well, I'm starving, yes. Being arrested twice, no one thought to feed me today. So sure, but I'd like to go home, so if it's all the same to you, maybe we can stop for something quick—takeout, a drive-thru…" She rubbed her arms, and even he could feel the chill of the night.

"I'm not talking about tonight," he said. "But yeah, I'll pick something up for us while we drive back. I mean dinner back in Livingston, maybe tomorrow? I'll take you out for that date I promised."

She furrowed her brow, confused. "You mean after all this today, all your digging into my background and being responsible for me being arrested, the spotlight shining on me for a crime I didn't commit because you thought I was lying and hiding something, you expect I'll forget it and go out for dinner with you?"

He could feel this going badly. "Well, when you put it like that, I'm sorry, Chloe. But, look, at least now you don't have to hide. We've cleared your name and made these bullshit charges go away, so you don't have to worry about something else coming out or pretending you're someone else…"

By the way she was staring at him, he wondered whether she would forgive him. "You want me to thank you for today?" She sounded so accusing.

"I want you to accept my humble apology and know that I never believed for a minute that you did what they said."

She seemed to consider that. Then those damn irresistible dimples popped. "You know, Luke, if you weren't so damn cute and if I didn't like your family as much as I did…"

"Is that a yes?"

"Barring any fights on the drive back, sure," she said, resting her hand on the door of the car. "Dinner tomorrow. But you're a long way from forgiven."

Just then, he spotted the sheriff walking out of the building, looking both ways, and crossing the street toward them. He walked around the front, and he could feel Chloe tense beside him, yet the sheriff didn't pull his gaze from Luke as he said, "Can I have a word with you?"

Luke looked down at Chloe. "Get in the car and wait. Give me a minute with him."

She only nodded and slid inside, and he closed the door and took a step over to the sheriff, who was now standing on the sidewalk. The man only glanced once to Chloe, who was belted in the passenger side, then back to Luke.

"I hope there're no hard feelings," the sheriff said to him. "This wasn't personal."

"Maybe for you it wasn't, but for Chloe Welch, you ripped her life apart." He wondered why the sheriff was there.

"Look, I understand you're in the military, and maybe you know how these things work, how policies dictate we have to run things. I swear, I really believed she lied about a lot of things."

Luke wondered what had been said to the sheriff, by the way the man looked away.

"You know Bessie Armstrong saw Chloe walking her dog, saw her witness the smoke and the fire, then saw Dirk Randall coming out of the Millers' house. You know too that she refused to come forward. You know Dirk Randall is guilty. You never had statements, did you, from the neighbors, the complaints?"

The sheriff glanced away and then back to him. "We did, but they were presented by the TX Group, their investigators, from all the property owners who had sold out and moved on. There were a lot of them, all notarized. Every one of them said exactly the same thing, word for word."

So it was a lie. "You mean like the same statement, copied and pasted? Yet you used it anyway even though you knew Dirk Randall and the company wanted all suspicion off him, and the only way to do that was to have someone else charged. That's sloppy on your part, Sheriff —or is it that you were told where to direct your investigation? You were to see to it that Chloe Welch was charged and convicted so the community could have their justice."

The sheriff glanced away.

"What do they have on you?" Luke said.

There it was, something he couldn't hide. Luke had figured it out. Yet the sheriff said nothing. "You should head back," the man finally told him. "Hope we don't have the pleasure of meeting again." He took a step back and started around the front of the Mercedes.

"Sheriff, what they have on you must be pretty bad, and you know they'll use it again," Luke said.

The sheriff stopped walking, his back still to him. He glanced over his shoulder without turning around. "I'm sure in your line of work, you or your team have made mistakes that cost a life. But mistakes happen. Is it better to destroy a man's career over one mistake or to make sure it never happens again? Let's be clear: Bessie Armstrong would never come forward. And now she's been made an offer she can't refuse."

He wasn't sure what he was saying. He'd have given anything to know what the huge corporation and Dirk Randall had on the sheriff. He figured he'd done something bad, or maybe his department had, and he was covering it up.

"It's going to come out, you know," he said.

The sheriff turned around. "Maybe it won't."

"What did you do? Who died? Was it someone who shouldn't have? A bad shooting?"

The sheriff only pulled in a breath. "Every police department across this country hides its mistakes. A bad shot, a mistaken arrest. Whatever it is, it's buried, and the file the public sees tells a different story."

"So you're now a puppet for the TX Group."

The sheriff made a face and nodded. "Let me tell you about the TX Group. They get where they are by having dirt on those they need to. Even if what they have comes out, it won't be accidental, and there are hundreds of others they have something against. This is bigger than you and me, Luke. So, again, Ms. Welch is free to go, and this case is closed. Any loose ends have already been taken care of."

He didn't know why he was struck with that off feeling again. "So they got to Bessie, or did you?"

The sheriff took another step toward him. "By this time tomorrow, a demolition crew will be on that block, clearing out all the debris. The last of the residents will be gone by morning. She's been relocated, and the community will get its jobs, and life will move on. The town of Cody will have a lot of happy households because there will be a wave of new construction jobs. Many will be brought in from out of state. Crime will increase, but life moves on." The sheriff rested his hands on his duty belt.

Luke knew that was all he was going to get. "You really think it's that simple."

The sheriff made a face. "There's nothing about it that's simple. I think you know that," he said. Then he spat on the ground, and when he turned and walked away, Luke said nothing else.

He strode to the driver's side and climbed in beside the redhead he'd once known intimately well.

"What was that about?" Chloe said.

"I guess that was the sheriff's way of apologizing for what happened today," Luke said, glancing only once to her as he started the car, pulled his seatbelt on, and pulled away from the curb. He drove to the end of the street. "So what do you figure, burgers or chicken?"

"Now, why don't I believe you? Pretty sure he said a lot more than that." She gestured to the blinking sign of a drive-thru burger place. "Burgers it is, I guess."

He pulled in and stopped behind two cars waiting to order, and he looked over to this smart, beautiful woman he'd spent the most incredible weekend with. "You really are beautiful, Chloe."

Her dimples popped again, and she slowly slid her gaze over to him. "And you're changing the subject. Just know this, Luke: You spent the day digging into my life, so I have a lot of catching up to do. How many secrets do you have that your family is just waiting to share?" She started laughing and reached over to touch his arm. "Oh, this is going to be so much fun."

A car honked behind them. It was their turn to move. He realized his family would likely offer way too much about him, which would be embarrassing but would be seen as payback.

"Just don't get too much enjoyment at my expense," he said, and she laughed again softly, a sound he thought he really could get used to.

"Life's challengers are not supposed to paralyze you,
they're supposed to help you discover who you are."

BERNICE JOHNSON REAGON

"Why are we here, again?"

Luke pulled his arms over his chest and took in his brother Marcus, who was still wearing his sheriff's uniform, having just pulled in in his cruiser. The dust settled in the parking lot of the concrete building surrounded by wire fencing. He heard barking from the back.

"Trying to make something right," he said.

Marcus pulled off his shades and joined Luke beside his old pickup. He'd called Marcus and told him to get his ass down there because he needed his help, and now his brother was staring at him as if he'd lost his mind. He gestured toward the building. "This is an animal shelter. I don't understand—making what right? Again, why am I here?"

Luke gestured to the front glass doors, but Marcus just stood there as if he had no intention of moving. "I need your help. That I have a sheriff for a brother means they'll waive the adoption period, so I can walk out of this shelter with a dog today instead of waiting."

He thought his brother was going to laugh for a moment. Then Marcus shook his head. "What the hell do you want with a dog? You're never here. You can't have a dog, because someone else will end up looking after it. And if you tell my kids, they'll want one. No, seriously. Get in your truck. Let's get out of here."

He finally reached out and slapped Marcus on the shoulder. "It's not for me, it's for Chloe, so stop worrying. You'll have no responsibility here."

His brother fell in beside him as he started walking to the door, but again he was shaking his head. "You're getting Chloe a dog? Seriously, there are better presents, ones that don't lift a leg on your furniture."

He only angled his head to Marcus as they walked into the shelter.

The lady behind the front desk tossed them an easy smile. "What can I do for you?" she said as she stood up. Her cheeks were round and her hair dark and short.

Marcus said nothing, only gestured to Luke with his thumb.

"Can I see the dogs you have up for adoption?" Luke said.

"Sure thing! We have quite a few. They're all out back. Just head through those doors there and follow the noise. Are you looking for any particular breed of dog?" She dragged her gaze from Luke to Marcus, who just lifted his hands, though at least he hadn't walked out. Luke knew his brother was still furious over how the Wyoming sheriff had made him look like a fool.

"Nope, just want to see what you have," Luke said, then tapped the counter and started walking to the back.

He pushed open the door and took in the line of kennels outside. There were so many of them, a little beagle who was sitting, staring up, shaking, and one that looked like a big Malamute back in the shade.

"I thought you were going to take her to dinner?" Marcus said as Luke walked, continuing to look at the dogs.

"I am. I plan on it," he said. He would show up with a dog and then ask her out that night.

"So why the dog? Seems overkill to me." Marcus walked behind him as he looked in each kennel. He could hear in his voice that he thought this was a bad idea.

"She had hers taken away in Wyoming over the Randall thing. She had a mutt, some little terrier. I had to Google it to figure out what it was. She loved that dog, and watching her talk about it, I just figured I could try to fix some of what was done to her—what I did, and you too."

His brother's smile was gone. He just stared at the cages and dogs before dragging those blue eyes over to Luke. There it was, the guilt. "Look, I feel horrible over what happened when Sheriff Kolter showed up with that warrant. That was the first time I've ever had to deal with that kind of underhandedness. I'm still kicking myself, because I know what a legitimate interstate warrant looks like, and I wish I could go back and have a second look now. You can be damn sure that'll never happen again. If there's ever a next time, I'll be picking up the phone and questioning the legality of every dotted i and crossed t."

Luke could hear the regret in his brother's voice. He wanted to remind him that even Karen had said someone would have to really look to see the difference. Evidently, Sheriff Kolter had known what he was doing.

"Well, that's the reason you're here, because you can help make it up to her. I'll make sure you get some credit so you're not in the doghouse, so to speak. That you went all official on her, turning from friendly Marcus to the sheriff who saw her as a criminal, it has her feeling about you the way Mom still feels about Harold."

His brother flinched. Even though Harold had been doing his job, personal was personal, and Luke could see it in the shadows of his mom's face. She was trying to tell herself she had to forgive him, that he'd done it only so things wouldn't have been worse for her.

His brother glanced away, then shook his head. "Charlotte went over to see Chloe. We're still trying to wrap our heads around her not being Misty. Just saying, it seems we as a family attract this. But Charlotte was adamant that we have to have her over to the house with everyone so the family can show her that nothing has changed. Then there's Suzanne. Harold said she wants Chloe to file a formal complaint about that sheriff."

"And you're okay with that?"

Marcus dragged his gaze over to him. "I'll even help her start the paperwork. If we want anything to change in this country, then people like Sheriff Kolter have to go. It's all I can think to do to tell her I'm sorry."

Luke realized Marcus held on to so much frustration and anger, something he suspected he was feeling more and more, having to wade in and deal with the truly ugly parts of humanity, the lying, the cheating, the taking. But not on the level that Luke did, and he hoped his brother never had to.

He made himself look away. "So I heard Suzanne is still giving you the gears about working for the sheriff's office." He took another step, walking past each of the cages, seeing all the dogs no one wanted.

Marcus let out a sigh. "She's not joining. She can push all she wants to, but it's not happening. Told Harold to figure out a way to steer her in another direction. Planning on moving Therese, too—you know, the lady who took over Charlotte's job? Well, she's good, so I plan to send her for some training and give her the open deputy job that used to be Lonnie's." Marcus angled his head as they took in a group of little bulldog puppies, four of them yipping away, climbing over each other with their stocky bodies and huge paws.

"So is that your way of giving your wife her job back?"

Marcus dragged his gaze over to him again, unsmiling. "Even though Therese is really good, the way she got the job was wrong, with the council overstepping because Charlotte had a baby. Charlotte swallowed it and didn't complain because she knew I was having to deal with all the overreach from the council and mayor. Well, not this time. Even though I love that she's home with Cameron and Eva, and being there for me, her job was a part of herself that she loved. So yeah, she's getting her job back." Marcus gestured to the pups. "You should get her the gray one."

Luke stared at the little bulldog pup, which would grow into a powerhouse. There was something about those eyes, the way it was pawing at the fence where his brother was standing, looking down at it.

"A puppy," Luke said. "He looks like a scrapper."

All Marcus did was grunt. "He's perfect—for you and her."

# Seventeen

His truck rumbled before he parked and turned off the engine, taking in the bungalow, its curtains drawn and blinds closed. He wondered how long it would be before Chloe felt comfortable again, considering hiding for so long had likely become second nature to her.

The puppy was climbing on the seat, and he lifted the little guy—or, rather, girl.

"Well, too late to take you back, so she'd better like you."

The puppy licked his face as he closed the door and held the wriggling bundle up the walkway. He pulled open the screen and knocked, then waited one second and then another. There it was, the slight flutter of the curtains, then the footsteps. He listened to the two dead-bolts being unlocked, and then the door opened. He took in her wide eyes as she pulled the door open further.

"Luke, what the...?" She gasped as he held the puppy out.

He didn't have to ask to come in. She just stepped back, and he let the door close behind him as he handed the puppy to her. "She's yours. I stopped at the pound and picked her up, so if you decide you don't want her, it's too late to take her back, so I'll be stuck with her—and Marcus has already pointed out that I can't have a dog because I'm gone at a moment's notice and someone else will end up looking after her."

She was laughing, and the puppy was licking her face, tail wagging. Her amber eyes reached out to him without the shadow of hurt he realized had likely always been there. "You got me a puppy? Why? How? This is crazy…"

Damn, those dimples of hers eased the tightness in his chest that had been there from the moment he'd walked out of the shelter with the pup, leaving Marcus to deal with the lady and see to it that the waiting period was waived.

"I'll never forget your face when you talked about BJ, the way he was taken from you. I know she can't replace your other dog, but…" He shrugged.

She put the puppy down and walked over Luke, one step, two, then rose on her tiptoes and pressed a kiss to his lips. She pulled back slowly, and for a moment he didn't know what to say, remembering what it was like to have her touch him, kiss him. He watched as the puppy squatted on the floor.

He winced.

"Oh, no you don't!" Chloe ran after the puppy.

Luke took in the hardwood and the old carpet in the living room, remembering what Marcus had said.

Chloe was already holding the dog, and she strode into

the kitchen and tossed him a roll of paper towels. "Clean it up for me, and I'll take her outside. What's her name?" She was scratching the puppy, who was licking her face again. She grimaced. "Oh, we're going to have to work on that."

Luke ripped off several sheets and tossed them on the ground. "It's up to you to name her," he said as he squatted down, wiping up the mess. He stood and walked into the kitchen.

"Garbage is under the sink," she said. "I guess I'm washing my floor again, aren't I...Lucy? How about Lucy?"

She strode to the back door as he tossed the paper towel in the garbage and then washed his hands. The back door closed, and he could hear her encouraging the puppy and clapping. Yeah, he'd scored big time there.

He walked to the door, taking in the sparseness of the house and how dark it seemed, all closed up. Looking out the back, he watched as Chloe checked the gate at the side of the fence. The puppy was running around the yard.

"I guess that needs to be secured better," Luke called out. "I'll walk the perimeter and find any holes, seal them up for you so Lucy can't get out."

"You know, Luke, I'm not really angry with you, if that's what this is about," she said.

He didn't know what to say for a moment. As he took in the redhead, awkwardness lingered. Having been with her on her worst day, he sensed all pretense was gone between them.

"I'm responsible for what happened," he said. "As has been pointed out to me, I don't know how to be happy. I've been fighting for so long, seeing the bad in everyone, that I see shadows where there aren't any."

Chloe pulled in a breath and glanced away, uncomfortable. "You said I was hiding something, and you were right. I was. But it was my secret, and you just wouldn't let up. So yeah, you pushed when you shouldn't have, and I'm angry about that, considering you have secrets too, Luke. Should I push with you, or do you have a right to them?"

She didn't pull her gaze. He didn't know how to explain to her that she was right to a point.

"Should I apologize?" he said. "Maybe I should, for how I went about it, but I can't apologize for the outcome. You don't have to hide anymore. You don't need to have your blinds and curtains closed so no one can see in. You don't have a sheriff and a county coming after you anymore just because you did the right thing. You don't have to pretend to be someone else—and take it from me, that isn't easy. You're right about me, though. I went into the special forces to make a difference, and I never know where I'm going to be sent with my team. I'll be gone at a moment's notice for months at a time, with no idea when I'll be home. I'm not the family guy my brothers are. I never will be."

He wasn't sure what to make of her expression.

"What are you doing, Luke? Sounds to me if you're pointing out all the reasons you can't be, as you said, happy. Is that what you're doing?" She angled her head.

"No, I'm just…" He stopped talking when she lifted a brow. He remembered the deal with his mom, the fact that his family would never stop trying to find a way for him to have his own kind of happiness. "Sorry, maybe I am. This is unchartered territory for me. There's something about you, Chloe. Considering we've already had a weekend with no strings and I've seen you naked, maybe I'm going about this all wrong."

She rested her hand on his bare arm and slid it up to the sleeve of his navy shirt. "How about dinner here?" she said. "You can help me secure the yard so Lucy can't get out, and you'll let me ask you all about the Luke that hides himself from everyone."

Maybe that was what he feared more than anything. He lifted his gaze and let out a rough laugh, knowing he could walk out the door and keep pushing her away, but he'd never be able to stop thinking of her and wondering what if. And that terrified him.

"You may decide I'm too much, you know. There are some things I can't share, not even with my family."

She seemed to consider, then nodded. "Fair enough. So how about this? National security is off the table, but anything else is fair game."

He wondered whether she had any idea what she was asking. "You may not like what you hear. I'm not a squeaky-clean choir boy."

She only inclined her head as she picked up the puppy, which was pawing at her. "If I was interested in a choir boy, Luke, I wouldn't have invited you in."

Her lips quirked, and he spotted the teasing light he'd seen in her eyes during that weekend he'd spent with her. He couldn't help himself from leaning in and kissing her.

When the puppy pawed at him and licked his face, he pulled back. At Chloe's soft laughter as he ran his hand over the puppy, he wanted to thank his family for putting her right in his path.

"Elaborate," Suzanne said, "because I've known Chloe as Misty for so long, yet I swear I've never seen her so happy. We know you've been staying over, so does this mean…?"

Luke was pouring a glass of wine for Chloe, and he could hear her laughter from the living room. Suzanne groaned and rested her hand on her lower back as she strode over to him, wearing an oversized yellow sundress, her hair pulled back.

"You okay there?" he said.

"Yeah, just the baby, the joys of being pregnant. Everything hurts. But don't change the subject. We're talking about you and Chloe." She angled her head and then smacked his chest when he laughed softly under his breath.

"Ow! Geez, Suzanne, dial back the aggression. Or is this how you keep Harold in line?"

His sister had always been tomboyish, and he was having trouble picturing her as a mom—which she would soon be, considering how their own mother was fussing over her.

"Harold is fine," Suzanne said. "You're the only one I do that to, because you like it." She shrugged.

"Sure, with guys, when I can hit back, but you're my sister." He screwed the cap back on the wine.

"I remember well the black eye you gave me…"

"You were twelve, and I wasn't much older," he said. "Besides, isn't this about you having your nose in my business, spying on me, really?"

Suzanne made a rude noise. "I wasn't spying. I was doing my due diligence, driving past Owen and Tessa's, and I just happen to have seen your truck parked there every morning. Combined with the fact that Mom says you haven't been home, I guess that means I can put you and Chloe down as officially together. You two will continue showing up for family night, and Mom will finally get you out of the house, and we won't have to find someone else for you, because we rather like Chloe. You're perfect for each other."

What was he supposed to say to that? Whenever he was with Chloe, he didn't want to leave. He couldn't not touch her, not kiss her, and he thought he could listen to her voice all night. Now it was him checking the windows and pulling the curtains closed again, because he was the one still seeing ghosts. There were just too many bad things out there.

But that was one secret he knew Chloe understood, and he figured she wouldn't share it. His family had some idea, but if they had only known what haunted him in his head, he wondered whether they still would have put Chloe in his path.

"It's what you wanted, isn't it?" he said. "So give

yourself a pat on the back and take the win, but you're not getting a blow by blow, because I don't kiss and tell."

"Chloe said you rebuilt the entire back fence in her yard."

He lifted a brow, as his sister didn't appear to have heard him. "Lucy needed a safe place that she couldn't get out of. Considering I gave Chloe the puppy, it was my responsibility to make sure she had a secure yard."

He could hear the laughter in Marcus's own yard out back, knowing the puppy was a source of entertainment for the kids and half the family. He'd already heard the kids pleading with Marcus too many times that they needed their own puppy.

"You're being domesticated, Luke."

He lifted the glass of wine and reached for his own beer. That was word for word what his mom had said, along with instructions not to blow it.

He heard Chloe, Charlotte, and Jenny talking as they stepped into the kitchen. Luke handed Chloe her glass of wine and couldn't resist leaning in and kissing her. Everyone was suddenly quiet, and when he pulled back, he could see them all watching.

"Okay, show's over," he said. "Who's barbecuing tonight, anyway, since Owen's not here?"

Then he heard a car door and voices.

"It's Owen and Tessa. They're back!" Jenny said. She was already walking to the front door along with Suzanne and Charlotte.

Chloe suddenly appeared nervous, as she hadn't moved.

"What's wrong?" he said.

She flicked her amber eyes up to him. Her peach halter sundress looked stunning on her, and he realized something about being with her centered him. "You know that Owen and Tessa still know me as Misty. They don't know about anything that happened…"

"Oh, I see. You're worried about what they're going to think."

She only shrugged, a motion he'd seen too many times over the past week. There were so many things she hadn't been able to shake, and he wondered how long it would take for her not to immediately worry about people thinking the worst of her.

"Did anyone here tell you to get out, or did everyone stand behind you?" he said.

She frowned and furrowed her brow. "So you think I'm silly for worrying."

He settled his beer on the island, then took her wine from her hand to rest beside it. Out front, his family was laughing. He rested both his hands on her bare arms, running them down and pulling her closer to him.

"No, not me, not ever me, but if I have to keep telling you, I think everyone here has already shown you they're in your corner. What happened to you in Cody will never happen again."

He could tell by the flicker of worry in those amber eyes that she was likely trying to convince herself of what he was saying.

"You know what I've wondered, Luke?" She settled into his arms, pressing all that softness against him as she looked up to him.

"What's that?"

"Bessie, the old woman next door. I know you told me she moved to Jackson Hole, where her son is, but you never told me how you found out or how she's doing. I don't know. Even after everything that happened, she crosses my mind every now and then."

Luke pulled in a breath, thinking of the call from Jess the day after they'd gotten back. The old woman had been taken out of her house by the sheriff's deputies while the bulldozers pulled in, and her son had driven all night to pick her up. She'd been given a court-ordered settlement for her property, only eighty cents on the dollar, and the TX Group had wasted no time in laying down the cement.

"I'm sure she'll be fine with her family," Luke said, "just like you are here with us. A new start, a new beginning. Just think: Sometimes bad things have to happen to get you to something good."

By the way her brows knit, she didn't agree. She went to pull back when he heard the squeak of the door and the voices of his family.

"So you're saying everything I went through was a good thing?" Chloe said.

He was treading in dangerous territory. He ran his hands over her arms again. "Well, if you hadn't, you wouldn't have been in Greece, we wouldn't have met, and you wouldn't be standing in my arms right now."

There were those dimples he loved.

"Well, Mr. O'Connell, that was a good save," she said.

He couldn't resist leaning in and kissing her.

T he puppy had fallen asleep about the same time Cameron had, Luke thought.

As he sat outside in Marcus's backyard, the sun had already set, and he could hear the soft voices of his family drifting from the house. His dad had pulled out a patio chair and sat down beside Owen, who had taken a minute to get his head around what had happened while he was gone on his honeymoon.

Marcus handed Luke another beer and sat in one of the other chairs between Harold and Ryan. As Jack reclined in the padded lounger with Karen leaning against him, Luke could just make out the state trooper standing off by the side.

"So are we going to talk about the elephant in the room?" Owen said. "You've had all this time to wrap your heads around what happened and ask questions, yet here I am, trying to understand how I didn't know Chloe was hiding something. I mean, now, as I look back, the signs are there. First there was the way she reacted when Tessa encouraged her to take that admin job at the high school, which had better pay and was practically being handed to her. And maybe I did wonder about how closed-up her house was, with the double locks, the blinds, the curtains, even when Tessa went over. I called out to her a few times when I saw her at the store, and she didn't turn around. Now I can see, even though it was—"

"Explained away?" Luke jumped in before Owen could continue down the road of trying to see every clue he'd missed.

"Yeah, I guess that's it. I just can't believe it."

Luke could feel his dad watching him and knew he understood more about everything that had happened, just as he did.

"What about the fire and the family who were killed?" Owen said. "I know you said Dirk Randall got off and won't be charged, but does that mean the case is...?"

"He can't be charged, Owen, because he was acquitted," Karen said, jumping in. "But I guess, like you, I thought it never made sense, why he did it or what happened in that house. I mean, don't you all want to know? Because I do. A man like Dirk Randall with a company the size of TX behind him, what was he doing, walking into a house and burning it down? That makes no sense. He'd have people to do that for him. Am I not right?" Her head was resting against Jack's chest, and it wasn't lost on Luke the way Jack had been fussing over her. The man really loved his sister, and he'd been rather quiet that night.

"I did some digging," Marcus started as he leaned forward, his forearms on his knees, a beer dangling from his hand. "Sal Miller wasn't as squeaky clean as people thought. I guess because he died in that fire with his kids and his wife, no one was looking at him, but I did find a sealed juvie record on him. He started a fire when he was thirteen, burned down a barn in the place he grew up outside Dixon. The old man inside died. Then, in his early twenties, Sal became a volunteer firefighter in Plympton, where he met his wife before they moved to Cody. The thing is that when I started looking at the dates and records, it seems Sal Miller lived in four different counties in a six-year period, and each of those counties had unsolved arsons."

Everyone was staring at Marcus. He'd had no idea his brother had been looking.

"You're saying Sal Miller burned down his own house and killed himself and his family?" Harold said, looking at Marcus as if he'd lost his mind. "Is that what you've been doing for the last week, all this research?"

Marcus only pulled his hand over the back of his neck, exhaled, and sat up. "From the beginning, from the moment this all went sideways, it was on me. The minute Sheriff Kolter called me, I drove him right to Chloe to cuff her and let him take her across state lines. I was angry she'd lied, but I didn't know there was an entire backstory with a lot of players. I didn't take the time to vet that warrant or, worse, to think for a moment that she could be innocent.

"That case, as I look at it, had so many holes. There are only three ways to solve a crime: You catch someone in the act, you have a witness, or you find evidence. Unfortunately, in Chloe's case, as in many, the first thing the defense did was poke holes, destroy the witness's credibility. So that left no witness. And what was the evidence? An accelerant and a head injury to the wife.

No one bothered to look into the fact that Deanna Miller had consulted a divorce lawyer, and she was going after half of everything Sal owned. The sheriff conveniently left out that she had also been seeking a restraining order against Sal. This was not a happy couple.

"Luke, when you told me about the incidents with Sal looking in Chloe's bedroom window, taking photos, I have to tell you, I wouldn't have given him a pass just because he owned the house. No, there was a lot of evidence against Sal."

"You think Sal burned down his own house? That he killed his wife?" Owen said as if on the verge of laughing because of how ridiculous it sounded.

"I think the kids got trapped, and he couldn't get them out. He had screwed up, so he died with his kids. I do think he killed his wife. It may sound crazy, but think about it. But, at the same time, what was Dirk really doing there, and what did he see? Smoke was spotted shortly after, then a fire. Was he there about buying out Sal, and his timing was just off? Maybe. Or maybe Dirk was planning on pointing the finger at him too, and it backfired. I did find that the TX Group made several offers to buy out Sal Miller and the houses he owned on that block. Dirk was turned down six times."

"You didn't hear this from me," Jack started, and Karen only turned her head, resting it against his chest. "Dirk Randall is currently being investigated by the securities commission for fraud. As for the sheriff, a video is going to be leaked this week documenting a bad shooting on the highway, a man who was trying to put down a bull. Sheriff Kolter is on video shooting the man in the back…"

"Bessie's husband," Luke said.

Jack looked over to him. He wondered how he'd found out, but then, this was Jack.

"So she gets her justice, does she?" Luke said. "But not her property back."

Jack said nothing else.

By the way Karen settled against her husband, she knew more. "Nope, that big goliath, the TX Group, gets its development," she said.

"It's not my state, Karen," Jack said, having likely heard an earful from her already.

"So how is it that the securities commission is investigating Dirk Randall?" Ryan asked.

Luke realized Jack had been making more than a few phone calls.

"I suspect they had a tip to point them in the right direction. He'll have to announce his resignation from the TX Group and will walk away disgraced but not impoverished."

Raymond stood up and looked down at all of them. "So it seems you made some justice happen," he said. "Marcus, let yourself off the hook. You're a good sheriff. Jack, you pulled some strings so Dirk loses the TX Group, but you're right that the development can't stop. Sheriff Kolter will likely face some charges, but no one will really know what went on in that house before it burned down. There will always be more goliaths out there, but one thing I know well is having to hide, and Chloe won't have to do that now. You make me damn proud every day, every one of you, because each of you in your own way is making a little corner of this world better. That's what I see. It's what I know."

Luke didn't know what to say. He'd never considered that.

His dad was staring down at Karen, who was still resting against her husband. Jack had wrapped his arms around her and pressed a kiss to her head, and by the way Raymond smiled at the two of them, Luke realized there was something else.

"You know," his dad said, "we could all use a little more good news. You told your mom and me earlier…"

Karen looked up at them all. "Jack and I are having a baby."

Jack gave a proud papa's smile as he kissed Karen's cheek again, and Luke looked over to his feisty, fiery sister as everyone shouted their congratulations. He stood and strode over, then bent down and kissed her on the cheek before tapping Jack on the shoulder.

"That's great, you two," he said. "You know what? I think I'm going to grab Chloe and that sleeping pup and head out."

As he strode across Marcus's backyard toward the house, hearing the laughter behind him, he realized his dad was right. In their own ways, they really were trying to make things right.

Turn the page for a sneak peek of
*BROKEN PROMISES coming next in THE O'CONNELLS*
*Available in print, eBook & Audio*

**She gave her daughter up. Now she wants her back.**

**What do you do when a woman shows up on your doorstep, suddenly wanting her daughter back?** Never in a million years did Marcus and Charlotte O'Connell expect to be faced with this kind of dilemma, but when Reine Colbert is released from prison, she shows up at their house, demanding they return her daughter, Eva.

Worse is the fact that Sheriff Marcus never received a courtesy call from the prison or parole board to warn him that Reine was about to be released. As far as he and Charlotte were concerned, they had followed Reine's wishes, adopting her daughter so she could serve her time, knowing Eva was loved and in a good family. But now she's changed her mind, and she believes Marcus is somehow responsible for her lost years with her daughter.

Though Marcus and his siblings step in to talk it through with Reine, who has been given a raw deal, little Eva is the one caught in the middle of the tug of war.

Will the O'Connells be able to reason with a woman who has no reason to trust anyone? Find out in a novel about secrets, hurts, lies, and the true of meaning of family.

# Broken Promises

## CHAPTER 1

She was thirty-one years old, and she had a daughter, a tattoo she would never be able to remove, eighteen dollars and forty cents in her pocket, and a prison record that would keep her from ever having anything else. Reine Colbert wondered when she hadn't felt this hollow ache that had become a part of her, of who she was, an anger that had only grown deeper, so much that it burned her with every breath she took.

She stared at the brick homes, sidewalks, and grass lawns of picture-perfect suburbia, with flowers planted in front of porches that welcomed visitors, family, and friends with glasses of lemonade, laughter, and small talk.

But that life wasn't for someone like her. That life had been ripped from her. Reine had once had a husband, a daughter. She'd once felt joy. Now she felt only anger.

It hurt more than anything to feel she was supposed to be thankful that she got to breathe the same air as people who had homes, lives, and freedom. Wasn't that exactly what her parole officer had said after he finished grinding her into the ground as she sat in his dingy office, realizing he didn't see her as human? He'd stared at her file instead of her, making it clear she'd never matter. She'd better learn her place, keep her nose clean, take what was offered. And he didn't want to hear any complaints or whining about anything, because rights were something she didn't have.

*No drugs, no liquor, no weapons.*

And the last, which had nearly choked her, was *no respect.* That was something she wasn't entitled to anymore. She'd been officially categorized as a person with no rights and no dignity, and she was terrified, as she stood on the concrete sidewalk, seeing weeds sprouting up between the cracks here and there, staring at a house, that what she was doing now could have her right back behind bars.

It would take just one call from someone who mattered, even though that would be cruel. Then again, cruelty had become familiar to her, and it was a quality she saw in everyone now.

Someone was watching her. This was that feeling prison had taught her, the one that had kept her alive and breathing. She waited a second before turning to see a woman with long dark hair across the street, staring.

Reine pulled at her old hoodie, lifting the hood over her shoulder-length dark hair even though it was mildly warm out. She made herself look away, around and up the street to see what could be coming at her. It was a quiet morning, and cars were parked in front of most of the houses. The sheriff's cruiser was in the driveway as the early sun topped the horizon.

She reminded herself she couldn't keep standing there, as someone would call the cops, and she'd be questioned, told she didn't belong. Reine made herself take one step and then another, hoping whoever was watching her would let her be instead of hitting her with the knowledge that she didn't belong there.

She kept moving in sneakers that were so worn she could feel each pebble she stepped on, but the pain was welcome as she walked up the sidewalk toward the two-story craftsman. Her legs were shaking, and her stomach was hollow, and Reine was very aware of the voices she could hear from inside.

The three front steps were painted gray. As she stepped up, she glanced down at the holes in her sneakers, and her heartbeat thudded long and loud in her ears. The hair on the back of her neck stood up. She wondered whether she'd ever shake that feeling of being watched, having to look over her shoulder, never feeling a moment's peace because of that deep ache in her soul, a reminder of everything she'd lost.

She took another step up, and the creak of the wood ricocheted through her. Her inhale was long and loud in her ears, her heart pounding, her hands sweating. One more step, and she knew she shouldn't be here, fearing the hand that would reach for her and pull her back, another living nightmare. Reine prayed for the day when that fear would truly leave her.

She fisted her shaking hand, feeling the sweat under her arms, down her back. Her blue jeans hung on her hips. The inside door was closed, and she stared at the screen mesh and lifted her hand to ring the doorbell, but instead she knocked on the white painted frame.

The sound was weak. Standing there, she wasn't sure

if anyone had heard her. She lifted her hand again when she heard voices and footsteps, and then the door opened. She'd never forget his face, his blue eyes, that all-cop look, even though she'd forgotten how tall he was, standing there in his sheriff's uniform.

For a moment, the silence hung thick in the air as she stared at the man who was responsible for everything she didn't have.

"Marcus, who's at the door?" someone called out. It was her voice, Charlotte.

Reine fisted her hands where they hung at her sides and stared through the screen that separated her from a man she felt only bitterness for. She took in the confusion that knit his brows, his hand on the door. He didn't answer his wife.

"Reine?"

Was he happy or angry? She couldn't tell from his deep voice. The screen was still closed, but then he pushed it open with a loud squeak. She heard the sounds of children and a voice she'd go to her grave knowing, because it was a part of her.

*Eva.*

"I don't understand. What…? How?" Marcus gestured toward her, and she could hear the confusion as his gaze bore down on her. "What are you doing here?"

She pulled her hood down. "Hello, Marcus," she said, her heart still hammering as she took in the gun holstered on his duty belt. Once, she'd never have believed she could come to hate that uniform, but now she did because of what it had taken from her.

He was still standing in the doorway, looking down at her. She knew she wouldn't be invited in. What, exactly, had she expected?

"Marcus, you didn't answer. Who's here…?" There she was, Charlotte, dressed for work in a brown deputy's shirt, her long dark hair pulled up. Her eyes widened as she stood beside Marcus, staring down at her. Charlotte's head just topped his shoulders, but they were both taller than her.

She was still trembling inside, facing the gatekeepers to her Eva. More guards, even though she was no longer behind the walls of a prison.

"Reine, what are you doing here?" Charlotte said. "I didn't know you were out. What's going on?"

Not even a welcome or a smile. That was something she expected, and there it was, the change in Charlotte's face, in her eyes. Gone was the caring, and the woman who'd taken her daughter was staring at her now in a way that told her she didn't want her here.

"I'm here to see my daughter," Reine said.

She didn't miss the exchange between husband and wife as if her fate was still up for debate, as if someone else decided what she could and couldn't do.

"You're out of prison?" Marcus said. "I don't understand. When did this happen?"

When had she become so aware of the tone of people's voices? Marcus's had an edge she hadn't expected.

"Yes, I'm out. I hope that's not a problem for you." She wondered if sarcasm dripped from her words. Maybe that was why she still hadn't been invited in.

Marcus stepped out of the house, forcing her to take a step back, something she was too familiar with. Then he took another and another, and she had to fight the urge to look back to see the steps she could fall down. He was right in front of her, his hands on his duty belt beside cuffs she hoped never to feel around her wrists again. But she refused to cower even though she was terrified of what he could do to her.

The screen door hadn't closed, and she knew Charlotte was still standing there, holding it open.

"Marcus, the children…"

Was that worry or fear in Charlotte's voice? Reine couldn't look at her because the sheriff was staring down at her with a hard expression, the only way people looked at her now.

"Go inside and take Eva and Cameron upstairs," he said without pulling his eyes from her.

Reine wasn't about to lower her gaze, either, even though looking a guard in the eye in prison would have been seen as challenging, threatening, with repercussions that ranged from having her privileges taken away to being beaten or tossed in isolation. Cruel was cruel, and that had been all she'd known for too long.

Reine made herself take a breath and instinctively fisted her hands at her sides again.

"Marcus, everything okay here? Jenny said there may be something wrong," came a voice from behind her.

She had to look away, down to the man looking up at her from the sidewalk in a park warden's uniform. He was tall, too, and from the way he looked at her, she could feel this going sideways.

"No, everything is fine, Ryan," Marcus said. "This is Reine. She's out of prison." He sounded so matter of fact, but the way he talked about her, as if addressing the weather or the news, ached.

From how the other man was looking at her now, she expected to be told to leave or maybe walked down the street by the two of them, out of the neighborhood, with a warning never to come back.

"You have my daughter, Marcus," she said. "I want to see Eva right now."

He lifted his gaze back to her sharply with an expression she didn't like, shaking his head. "I don't think that's a good idea, Reine. She's happy now, and she wouldn't understand. You just showing up here like this isn't good for her. It's confusing, and—"

"She's my daughter!" She thumped her chest with her fisted hand, cutting him off, and it felt so damn good to do it, because it was something she'd never have been allowed to do in prison.

His gaze snapped to the sudden movement, and she reminded herself she was in front of a cop, standing right on his doorstep. She needed to be careful not to be construed as threatening or aggressive, even though the words she wanted to say were screaming through her head. The anger that radiated through her was clouding her reasoning.

"No, Reine," Marcus said. "She's our daughter now. Charlotte and I adopted her. Did you forget it was your idea? Now you're showing up here without calling, demanding to see her. What is this?"

That was something else she'd become far too used to, being denied everything she loved. The lump in her throat threatened to choke her, and tears burned her eyes from the anger that was only swelling deeper, bigger, burning a hole right through her.

"This is about my daughter, Marcus. Mine. I gave birth to her, and she was taken from me…"

He lifted a hand, and for a moment she thought he would touch her, so she jerked her shoulder sharply away. He must have known, as he pulled his hand back. "I can see you're angry and hurt, but I really don't think right now is a good time," he said. "We'll talk, and maybe we can look at something down the road when you're a little more settled." His hand went to his duty belt again, and she felt the dismissal, knowing the other man was still standing there, watching her, maybe waiting for her to move too fast or do something he didn't like.

Reine didn't nod. This was too familiar, being told to leave. Then they'd circle the wagons and make sure Eva was moved further out of reach. She was shaking her head as she said, "No, I'm not leaving. I came to see my daughter, and you can't keep her from me."

"Reine, you're making this very difficult. I said no. What is it you really want here? What is this really about? If you were truly thinking of Eva's best interest, you wouldn't be here now, showing up without calling."

She tried to look past him, but he was right there, blocking the door. She lifted her chin and refused to look away from the hard blue eyes of the cop looking down on her. "What I really want is to have the life that was stolen from me. That's what I really want, Marcus. But I can't have that, and I have to live with the shitty hand I was dealt. I've already asked you, and you've denied me seeing my daughter. So hear me, Marcus O'Connell. I'm standing here on your doorstep, and you have my daughter inside, and I'm telling you I want her back. Not to visit, not to make an appointment so you can decide whether I can or can't see her. I want her back. She's mine." She was trembling and knew she should be terrified by the way he was staring down at her.

"No, absolutely not," he snapped.

She picked up the sharp edge in his voice and heard the creak of the step behind her, knowing her time was up. A hand would grab her and push her away.

She didn't think. She could feel the panic and the agony of her daughter being ripped away from her again. It was her sweet face, her image, and her name that had kept her sane, so she did the only thing she could think of. She opened her mouth and yelled, "Eva!"

"Lorhainne Eckhart is one of my go to authors when I want a guaranteed good book. So many twists and turns, but also so much love and such a strong sense of family."

(LORA W., REVIEWER)

New York Times & USA Today bestseller Lorhainne Eckhart is best known for writing Raw Relatable Real Romance where "Morals and family are running themes." As one fan calls her, she is the "Queen of the family saga." (aherman) writing "the ups and downs of what goes on within a family but also with some suspense, angst and of course a bit of romance thrown in for good measure." Follow Lorhainne on Bookbub to receive alerts on New Releases and Sales and join her mailing list at LorhainneEckhart.com for her Monday Blog, all book news, giveaways and FREE reads. With over 120 books, audiobooks, and multiple series published and available at all, retailers now translated into six languages. She is a multiple recipient of the Readers' Favorite Award for Suspense and Romance, and lives in the Pacific Northwest on an island, is the mother of three, her oldest has autism and she is an advocate for never giving up on your dreams.

"Lorhainne Eckhart has this uncanny way of just hitting the spot every time with her books."

(CAROLINE L., REVIEWER)

***The O'Connells:*** *The O'Connells of Livingston, Montana are not your typical family. A riveting collection of stories surrounding the ups and downs of what goes on within a family but also with some suspense, angst and of course a bit of romance thrown in for good measure. "I thought I loved the Friessens, but I absolutely adore the O'Connell's. Each and every book has different genres of stories, but the one thing in common is how she is able to wrap it around the family, which is the heart of each story." (C. Logue)*

***The Friessens:*** *An emotional big family romance series, the Friessen family siblings find their relationships tested, lay their hearts on the line, and discover lasting love! "Lorhainne Eckhart is one of my go to authors when I want a guaranteed good book. So many twists and turns, but also so much love and such a strong sense of fami-ly." (Lora W., Reviewer)*

***The Parker Sisters:*** *The Parker Sisters are*

*a close-knit family, and like any other family they have their ups and downs. Eckhart has crafted another intense family drama… "The character development is outstanding, and the emotional investment is high…" (Aherman, Reviewer)*

**The McCabe Brothers:** *Join the five McCabe siblings on their journeys to the dark and dangerous side of love! An intense, exhilarating collection of romantic thrillers you won't want to miss. — "Eckhart has a new series that is definitely worth the read. The queen of the family saga started this series with a spin-off of her wildly successful Friessen series." From a Readers' Favorite award—winning author and "queen of the family saga" (Aherman)*

**Billy Jo McCabe Mystery:** *The social worker and the cop, an unlikely couple drawn together on a small, secluded Pacific Northwest island where nothing is as it seems. Protecting the innocent comes at a cost, and what seems to be a sleepy, quiet town is anything but.*

*Lorhainne loves to hear from her readers! You can connect with me at:*

www.LorhainneEckhart.com
lorhainneeckhart.le@gmail.com

facebook.com/AuthorLorhainneEckhart

twitter.com/LEckhart

instagram.com/lorhainneeckhart

bookbub.com/profile/lorhainne-eckhart

pinterest.com/lorhainneeckhart

The Fallen O'Connell
The Return of the O'Connells
And The She Was Gone
The Stalker
The O'Connell Family Christmas
The Girl Next Door
Broken Promises
The Gatekeeper
The Hunted

## The McCabe Brothers

Don't Stop Me (Vic)
Don't Catch Me (Chase)
Don't Run From Me (Aaron)
Don't Hide From Me (Luc)
Don't Leave Me (Claudia)
Out of Time

## A Billy Jo McCabe Mystery

Nothing As it Seems
Hiding in Plain Sight
The Cold Case
The Trap
Above the Law
The Stranger at the Door
The Children
The Last Stand
The Charity

## The Wilde Brothers

The One (Joe and Margaret)
The Honeymoon, A Wilde Brothers Short
Friendly Fire (Logan and Julia)